Hounded

Terry Burns

Hounded

2014 Terry Burns
All rights reserved.

Chapter 1

There were no lights on in the small cabin.

Sam stepped inside, fumbled for a match to light the lantern, and turned up the wick. As the tiny flame blossomed, he saw her lying near the fireplace. He caught his breath, suddenly getting lightheaded. The room swam and he put out a hand for the small table to steady himself. Missing the table, he went to his knees.

He crawled over to her. Blood was everywhere. "Mama!" he screamed.

He cradled her head. Her eyelids flickered open. "Sam?" She reached up with a bloodstained hand. "Thank God, I was so hoping that I'd see you before … before …"

The sentence was lost in a painful sounding cough.

Sam looked at her wounds. She had been stabbed several times. Her simple homespun dress was soaked and a pool of blood surrounded her on the floor. It didn't seem possible she could have any left in her body.

"Who did this?" he croaked.

"Drifter," her voice was almost a whisper. "He had a marled eye with a scar leading through it. Big man, black hair and mustache. He was so evil."

She gave a couple of choking coughs, then a tiny smile.

He gathered himself to rise. "I better go for the

doctor."

She took a grip on his arm to prevent him from getting up, her smile becoming weaker. "There's no time. You'll bury me by your father, won't you?"

His face was a mask of shock and disbelief. "Bury you? No, no, you can't leave me."

"It's all right. I'm ready. I prayed that God would let me say goodbye and he did. He allowed me to hang on."

More coughing wracked her small body.

Sam cried openly now, the tears blurred his vision as they ran down the stubble on his cheeks. "No, it just can't be."

"The man tried to have his way me, but I fought. He didn't expect it, I think. I used my paring knife on him, cut him good on his cheek down to his neck, but then he took it away and used it on me."

She coughed again and then smiled. "He didn't get what he was after. I beat him out of that."

Sam's face became suddenly hard, his eyes burned in their sockets. "I'll get him. Those scars will make him easy to find."

Her eyes pleaded with his, "No! Let the sheriff handle it. I don't want you getting into trouble. You've always been a good boy. Let the law handle it. You hear me?"

His face softened. "Yes, Ma'am."

He always did as his mother wished, but he wasn't sure he could do it this time.

"One more thing…"

"Yes, Ma'am?"

"I know so often people lose their faith over the death of a loved one. Promise me you won't blame God. He isn't taking me; that bad man did that, but I

4

know he's ready to welcome me. I can feel it. Someone is here for me, they've been here with me, I've felt them waiting patiently, but I know they're here. You have to promise me you won't blame –"

She made a strange rattling sound. "Mama?"

No answer.

She was gone.

<>

Sam didn't know how long he sat there, cradling her head in his lap, rocking and crying as he held her close. He knew what he had to do, but he didn't want to do it, didn't want to say goodbye. His mother was his life, the only family he had.

Why hadn't he been there with her? Why wasn't he there to protect her and keep her safe when she needed him most?

He knew why. Since his father had died, Samuel Duncan had worked as a day hand on surrounding spreads or even done odd jobs in town as he made ends meet and took care of his mother. The little blanket spread had gone on the block some time ago, bought by a big neighbor who let them continue to live in their house since he had no use for it. Sam paid the rent by the day work he did for that rancher in return. It was a lot to ask of an eighteen-year-old.

Sam hadn't complained, somebody had to do it and hard work had been his life since he was a youngster. Hard work and scratching around to keep food on the table made him lean and tough as a rawhide rope.

It didn't make him anything special. Boys his age were riding with the cavalry and on trail drives, working as cowboys or in stores and factories. Girls even younger were getting married and starting families. Young people grew up fast on the frontier.

He knew that everybody was aware of how rough it had been for them and he really felt like people respected him for how he had stood up to a man's responsibility. He'd done his best to earn that respect and had just finished working roundup at the Anchor J. He'd hurried back, not wanting to spend another day without checking on his mother. He'd ridden through the night to get home. He wished he had started home earlier, or not worked that job … something … anything.

He knew why he hadn't been there . . . but it didn't help.

Light from the windows told him the sun was well up.

With a deep sigh he mustered the strength to get up. He had to bury her. He picked up the knife to cut some canvas from the wagon cover in the barn. It would make a suitable shroud.

He moved woodenly, as if in a daydream. His head didn't work and his chest felt as if it was locked in a vise. He was in such a state that he didn't even see the big man sitting his horse in front of the house.

"What's going on here, boy? How'd you get that blood all over you?"

Sam's head came up to look to where the voice had come from, trying to focus, trying to make sense of the words.

Sheriff Fancher's gun came out. "That looks like a bloody knife you're toting, boy. You best let it drop and keep your hand away from that gun."

The sheriff was from nearby Turkey Creek and had known Sam all his life, but apparently felt the knife couldn't be ignored.

"Knife?" Sam looked at it stupidly, as if seeing it for the first time. "Oh, I'm going out to cut a piece of canvas."

"Whatcha need canvas for, boy? Where's yore mama?"

The barrel of the sheriff's forty-five looked as big as a drainpipe and didn't so much as waver, but it barely rated a glance. Sam continued to stare at the knife trying to make sense of things. He remembered what he was doing.

"I need it to bury mama. She's dead."

"Dead?" Fancher thumbed back the hammer on his forty-five. "Maybe you best lift that hogleg out of that holster easy like with your left hand, and I ain't gonna tell you again to drop that knife."

Sam let both drop on the porch. "What're you giving me such a hard time for, Sheriff? I came home to find her all cut up; it's the worst day of my life."

Fancher extended his left hand as if warding Sam off. He made a sweeping gesture, keeping the pistol trained steadily. "You step away from those weapons, down to the end of the porch. I don't know what's going on here, but I shore enough aim to find out. And I can't check it out and keep an eye on you at the same time."

Sam moved down the porch and Fancher stepped down from his horse. A big man with a potbelly, he wasn't the lawman he had once been, balding and soft. He was still enough lawman to tote the badge, though, and he took the job seriously.

He tossed a pair of manacles to Sam. "You reach around that post and put these on, boy."

Sam reached around the rough cedar post and snapped the manacles on both wrists. He leaned against it and closed his eyes, the rough bark grating his cheek, "I told you I didn't do anything, sheriff. I found her that way."

"So you say. I ain't gonna keep telling you everything twice, son. You settle yourself down there and I'll get to the bottom of this. If I'm wrong, I'll apologize."

Chapter 2

Fancher was white when he came out of the house. "Kinda wish I hadn't already had my breakfast. It's sure not sitting good on my stomach right now."

Sam looked at him through haunted eyes. "She said it was a drifter, big man with a marled eye."

Sam was seated now, his hands hanging limply where they were joined on the other side of the pole, his legs straddling the pole hanging off the porch. "She said she marked him again with this knife, too."

The sheriff wet his bandana in the rain barrel, mopped his face and neck as he looked down on his prisoner. "You saying you come in after it was done and she talked to you?"

Sam nodded, but put no effort into it. "That's how it happened, Sheriff. She said she held on to say goodbye."

The big lawman put his hands on his hips as he looked down on Sam. "Son, that woman has been dead for some time, she ain't talked to nobody."

"I've been sitting with her a long time."

"How long?"

Sam looked up stupidly, "I don't know, time—" His voice trailed off and he looked helplessly at Fancher.

The sheriff didn't offer to take the cuffs off, but sat

down on the porch step as if his legs weren't supporting him. He waited for the boy to finish the sentence but finally decided he wasn't going to do it. The sheriff's face was devoid of color and he had beads of sweat on his forehead. "You didn't spend the night here?"

Sam's voice was flat, toneless, drained of all emotion. "I rode all night to get here. Got in before sunrise."

"Sun has been up a couple of hours, but I don't see no signs of anybody but you in there. Gotta admit though, it ain't like you...

Ain't like you at all."

Fancher pulled his bandana and wiped his face and neck again then looked down and shook his head. "You've always been a good kid, but I have to say from the looks of things, it looks an almighty lot like you were here all along."

He put the bandana back and looked intently at his prisoner, seeming to make up his mind, "The way it looks you two got in a fight and you killed her. When I rode up and caught you with her blood on you and the knife still in your hand, you went and invented this drifter feller."

He leaned over to look Sam right in the face. "How come you done it, boy?"

Disbelief was written all over Sam's face. "What reason would I have to kill her? Sheriff, you know me, you know I loved her. She was all the family I had, my whole world."

Fancher grunted. "There's no figuring some of the things people do." The lawman got up grimacing from the effort. "I see it all the time. People who are normal their entire lives wake up one morning and start acting like they've been grazing on locoweed."

It was beginning to seep through the fog that had enveloped Sam's head. He realized he was in trouble. His face became animated.

"Sheriff, I didn't do it, you've got to believe me."

The sheriff reached for the post to steady himself as he stepped to the ground in front of the porch, "It don't matter whether I believe you or not, boy; my duty is clear; I've got to go lock you up."

He brought out the keys to release the manacles. "You can tell it to the judge."

"Can't we at least get her buried first?" Sam got to his feet and offered his hands to the big man, hugging the pole.

"I'll send the undertaker out for her." Fancher unlocked the manacles, removed them from around the post and locked them behind Sam's back.

"I can't afford to pay the undertaker."

"Thought you said you just worked a roundup?"

"Oh ... oh yeah. But I got bills that are due."

"One thing at a time, son, one thing at a time."

Sam moved as if in a fog, as if he didn't understand what was taking place. He fought to focus, to make sense of things. He needed his wits about him and he needed to do it right now.

"For her, did you say? She wants to be buried next to my Pa here on the ranch."

"I'll tell him. Right now you got bigger things to think about."

Chapter 3

"That's a beautiful pattern." Sharon Delmar fingered the material on the bolt of cloth spread before her on the dry goods counter.

"I just got that in from Kansas City." Storekeeper Ray Bates leaned on the soft goods counter at the Turkey Creek General store. "It's the latest thing."

As the daughter of Colonel Robert Delmar, the largest rancher in the trade area, Sharon was one of his best customers. When she came in, she had his undivided attention.

He smiled. "That blue brings out the color of your eyes."

Sharon didn't need much help in that department. Her bright smile, trim figure and golden hair played a prominent role in the dreams of most of the cowboys in the area. The everyday, blue-flowered dress with white trim that she wore now was better by far than the Sunday-go-to-meeting clothes most of the area ladies had in their closets.

Sharon cocked her head to look at a young lady standing nearby. "Oh, I don't know, what do you think, Candace?" She draped the cloth across her shoulder to provide a comparison.

The storekeeper's daughter had been Sharon's friend her whole life, more by chance than by choice. There were few girls their age in the area, and they had just turned sixteen within weeks of each other. Tiny, with mousy brown hair and eyes and a shy smile that seldom peeked out, Candace was the oldest, but basked in the glow of her vivacious friend. The gingham dress she wore was plain, but the stitching was tight and precise, done by her own hand.

Candace came around the counter, arranged the cloth on Sharon's shoulder, then stepped back and looked. "Daddy's right, it really brings out the color of your eyes."

"You think so? How sweet of you to say." Sharon pushed it across to the storekeeper. "Give me five yards of it, Mr. Bates, and some of that white lace for trim."

The storekeeper moved quickly to comply.

The screen door banged open as Zeke Flagg rushed through. The tinkling of the bell of the bell on the door was unnecessary after the explosive sound of his entry. He slowed down to a brisk walk, the startled look on the faces of those in the store assuring him that he had their full attention. Zeke was the town gossip in Turkey Creek, living by converting his intimate knowledge of all that went on in the area into drinks and meals.

Zeke was a beanpole of a man, habitually unshaven, with a fragrance that bore mute testimony of a lifelong aversion to the benefits of soap and water; not a man one would want to spend time in close proximity to.

Ray looked up and said, "You're in a big hurry, Zeke. I figure that means you have some fresh news."

"I'll say I have." Flagg pulled himself erect, bolstered by the importance of his latest item of gossip. "But perhaps I should take care of my shopping first."

Ray understood the drill. In a town too small to have a newspaper, Flagg performed a valuable service, but one might say like a newspaper there was a subscription fee involved.

"Whatcha need?"

"I'm short of flour, sugar and some of that Arbuckles coffee."

"Better be mighty good news, that's a steep price." The storekeeper set the items on the counter. As per custom, Flagg knew not to reach for them until the value of the news he brought had been assessed.

The man looked at the items and weighed the value of his message. "And I could use a slab of bacon."

Ray's eyebrows rose. The man had a good sense of the importance of the items he carried about town, and with his curiosity rising, the storekeeper added the bacon to the order.

Flagg nodded, seemingly satisfied with the deal he had struck. "The sheriff just brought in Sam Duncan. He killed his mother, with a knife."

"What?" Ray had turned back to the task of measuring the cloth Sharon had ordered, but was so surprised that he lost his place. He turned to the little man, shock on his face. "I can't believe it."

Turning back, he had to start over, struggling to concentrate on the task.

Both girls had grown up with Sam. He had been sweet on Sharon for some time. "I don't believe that at all," she said indignantly.

Candace looked mad. "Something is wrong here. Sam loved his mother, he'd never hurt her."

"Sheriff caught him standing over her with a

bloody knife," Zeke said with authority. He looked forward to a great evening at the saloon, armed with this outstanding new material.

"Well, I'm going to go see about this." Sharon made a dismissive gesture to the storekeeper and turned for the front door. "Put that cloth on our bill." She looked back over her shoulder. "Candace, are you coming?"

Candace implored her father with her eyes, "Is it all right, Daddy?"

The storekeeper nodded, and she pulled her apron off and pulled her bonnet on as she rushed after her friend. Sharon was already out the front door heading across the dirt street under a full head of steam.

<>

"Crazy woman." Rafe Logan sat at the waterhole trying to put a couple of stitches into the knife wound on his neck.

He strained to see in the little shaving mirror. He'd rather go see a doctor, but the only one close by would surely get him in all kinds of trouble with the law. Fortunately, he had a full fifth of red-eye and used it liberally, mostly applying more of it to the inside than the outside. He'd done this before.

He grimaced as he touched the wound. "Pretty woman living out there all alone, you'd think she'd welcome a little attention. Instead, she goes off on me like a pistol with a busted trigger. Ain't no figuring womenfolk."

Logan took a long draw on the bottle, poured a substantial amount on the cut, then fought nausea as he pushed the needle through the skin and pulled it together. He did it again and again. Reapplying the alcohol inside and out between stitches.

It ain't pretty, he thought when he finished, but it'll hold.

He looked at it as closely as the small mirror would allow.

Another scar. If this keeps up I'm gonna start looking like a patchwork quilt.

Logan finished his work, then sat back to finish the bottle as well. A man with a habitually mean disposition, the neck wound was doing nothing to improve it. He stared deep into the fire, not even bothering to move when the wind shifted and blew the acrid smoke in his face. His liberally applied anesthetic was starting to work.

The enormity of what he had done was not something he would dwell on; in his twisted view, it was the woman's fault for not welcoming his advances. What he would dwell on was the fact that there had been nothing worth taking at the place. Well, almost nothing, he thought with an evil grin.

He suddenly felt the need to go to the bushes. He pulled the woman's Bible out of his saddle bags, hefted the book for a moment then tore out several pages. He smiled, Lucky find, paper is mighty hard to come by out here, particularly nice thin paper like this.

He moved out a ways from the campsite to take care of his pressing need, his mind on the next order of business. He was broke. He had to come up with something to give him a bankroll, but he hoped to get out of the area without being seen. He didn't think there was any pursuit, but couldn't afford to take the chance that he was wrong.

<><

Sam sat in the darkness of his cell, dumbfounded. Things had happened so fast he couldn't seem to sort them out in his head. This simply couldn't be happening.

The cell was real enough though, damp and dark and smelling of mold and sweat. No telling how many men had sat in here contributing to that smell, and he was doing his part to add to it now. Little light came through the barred window, too high to see out without something to stand on.

In the outer office, Sharon swept into the room like a tornado clothed in a dress.

"Hello, Sheriff, how are you today?" she said briskly as she walked through, headed straight for the back where the cells were located.

Candace was a diminutive shadow trailing silently in her wake.

"Now hold it right there, Miss Sharon, you girls shouldn't be in here," he whined. "I've got a killer locked up back there."

The sheriff would have undoubtedly gotten to his feet and removed his hat for a woman coming into the office. The fact that he did neither was mute testimony to the fact that he still looked on this pair as young girls in spite of the fact that females out west were generally married by the time they got to be this age. He didn't even bother to take his feet from the desk.

Sharon reluctantly stopped. She noticed he hadn't stood and was tempted to call him down on it. No, she thought, this is no time to get him out of sorts. She decided the best course of action was to work her naïve little country girl routine on him.

"Oh poo, Sheriff," Sharon purred, "Sam is no killer." She swatted at the air as if shooing away a troublesome gnat. "We've known him our whole lives."

She batted her dark eyelashes at the big lawman and gave him a smile that would have blinded a lesser man.

He wasn't charmed, wasn't fooled, but he was amused. "You think you're going to charm your way in there to see him, right?"

She cocked her head and fluttered her eyelashes at him again. "Why Sheriff, whatever are you trying to suggest?"

He gave them a fatherly smile. "I'm not suggesting anything, but if you girls want to go see him, you've got to go get the permission of the judge. I'm not sending a pair of impressionable young girls in to see somebody that folks believe is a cold-blooded killer. The Colonel would have my hide."

Sharon cocked her head and put her hands on her hips, "Sheriff, we're not children."

"Now how would I know that? Where's the dividing line? One day you're in school and playing with dolls and the next you're standing over a stove in some man's kitchen cooking with a passel of children hanging onto your skirt. Somebody oughta blow a whistle or something, you know, kinda warn us when it's happening."

Sharon smiled; she just couldn't see herself in such a role. How common. "Now you're being silly."

"Am I? I just know it ain't gonna be me letting you in there so you can quit making cow eyes at me."

"Oh, poo!" She spun and stormed out of the jail. "Come on, Candace, let's go find the judge."

Candace stood for a moment watching her go. Her friend was so hard to keep up with. Meekly she ducked her head, gave the sheriff a small smile and followed in her wake.

Chapter 4

The girls stomped across the dirt street, leaving a light cloud of dust swirling behind them, on a mission to find where the judge was sleeping off last night's indiscretions. The sheriff shook his head as a wry grin came across his face thinking what he had just released on the little man.

"What was that act you were doing with the Sheriff?" Candace rushed to catch up. "Flirting with a man old enough to be your father, you should be ashamed."

"I wasn't flirting, you goose. If I play the little country girl card, men usually do what I want them to. The Sheriff is just too far over the hill or it would have worked."

"You still should be ashamed, trying to manipulate him like that." Candace had watched Sharon pull that routine since they were little girls, had watched her get her way over and over, but didn't understand how she managed it. "I would never do that."

"I know," Sharon smiled sweetly, "and that's why I usually get my way and you still get treated like a little girl. You just don't understand how the game is played." She stopped and looked closely at her friend. "But perhaps someday you will."

They reached the batwing doors of the saloon and Sharon burst through them as Candace squealed, "You can't go in there!"

"Your friend's right," the man behind the bar said. "You can't come in here."

"I'm looking for the judge." Sharon squinted as her eyes adjusted to the dim light and she swept the room slowly looking at each face.

A cowboy registered interest and started to get up.

"Sit down, Jackie Don," the bartender said, "her daddy would have you for breakfast. That's the Colonel's daughter."

The cowboy hunched his shoulders as if he had suddenly been hit by an icy blast of wind and sat back down giving off a small whistle. "I ain't going head-to-head with the Colonel," he said to the man next to him.

Every cowhand in the room suddenly became totally preoccupied with their drinks, clearly pretending she wasn't even there.

Sharon ignored the exchange. Finishing her survey of the room she looked toward the doors up the stairs.

"Oh no you don't." The barman came out from behind the bar blocking her way. "Ain't no way you're going up there."

Her hands went to her hips again, a classic pose for her as a storm-cloud look settled onto her face. She spoke slowly, making each word distinct, "Then tell me where he is."

"He sure ain't up there." The bartender didn't want trouble with her any more than the cowboy did; he just wanted her out of there, and the faster the better.

"How would I know where he is this morning?" He jerked his thumb over his shoulder indicating the alley behind the saloon. "You might try out back, sometimes he don't make it all the way home after I lock up."

Sharon spun around and banged through the doors, nearly running over Candace, pausing as she tried to adjust to the bright sun again.

"Now where?" Candace backed up so fast she nearly fell.

"Out back," Sharon headed for the space between the buildings. "And if that doesn't work, to the boarding house."

Sharon lifted the hem of her skirt out of the dust as she walked and Candace did the same behind her. She slowed as she got to the back stairs, and in the shadows under the stairs she found her quarry. "Judge? Judge, can you hear me?"

The rumpled pile of clothes in the corner stirred and a pair of bleary eyes peeked out from under a soiled derby. "Who's there?"

She made no effort to get closer where he could focus on her; the stench was quite enough as it was. She pulled a small handkerchief out and held it to her nose. "It's me Judge, Sharon Delmar."

The pile made no effort to move, "What is it you want, Miss Delmar, can't you see I'm busy with my daily meditations?"

His head disappeared back into the pile. Sharon reached over and shook him, "Judge?"

"Who's there?"

"We've already done that. Judge we need your permission to go see Sam at the jail."

He refused to look up but merely made a couple of ineffectual swats at the air. "Do what you want; just leave me alone."

Sharon turned to Candace in triumph. "I'd say that constitutes permission."

Candace shook her head slowly. "Hardly, he hasn't got the slightest idea about what you asked him, much less what he was agreeing to."

"Oh poo, you're splitting hairs. The Sheriff said to get his permission, and he said for us to do what we want. That's clear enough."

<>

As soon as the girls left the office, the Sheriff got up and ambled into the back like a bear just up from hibernation. "Company coming, boy."

He opened the cell door to let Sam get to the washbasin. "You might want to spruce up a little, they're pretty little fillies."

"I thought you said they couldn't come in?" Sam stepped out to pour the tin basin full of cold water from the pail. He stripped to the waist revealing a muscular chest and tight stomach. The years of work made him more man than his age or his boyish features would suggest.

The sheriff leaned against the door jamb picking at his teeth with the fingernail of his little finger, "Oh, they'll be back, ain't no stopping that little gal when she gets her mind set on something. I was just covering my backside."

He seemed to get what he was mining for in his teeth and spit, "Let that old gin-soaked excuse for a judge take the heat if'n there is any. I don't think her daddy goes agin her wishes much either."

He grinned, "lessen he gets hot and puts his foot down. Ain't hard to figure how she come by her temperment."

Sam washed his face and upper torso, worked up a

good lather and then sponged it off. He was wiping off his face on the none-too-clean towel when a soft voice said, "My, my."

Sam looked over the towel into a pair of amused blue eyes. He fumbled to get his shirt back on.

Sheriff Fancher grimaced, "Now I told you girls …"

"Don't get yourself in a lather, Sheriff; we found Judge Larribee behind the saloon. I'm sure he said it was all right, didn't you think that was what he said, Candace?"

Candace trailed into the open cell block behind her friend, head down, clutching her hands together. "Yes, I'm sure it was," she mumbled.

"Well," the sheriff scratched the back of his head. "I oughta have it in writing or something."

Sharon continued to devour Sam with her eyes. "I agree, Sheriff, why don't you go over there and try to wake him up. See if you can get him to write something that's legible."

"Like I'm going to go off and leave you two in here alone with him. Sam, you get yourself back inside that cell. I got to at least get the bars between you two. If I ain't careful the Colonel may have my hide tacked up on his barn door yet."

Sam went back inside. He winced as he listened to the metallic clink as the sheriff turned the key in the lock. In the small space, it sounded to him like someone striking an anvil. He stood holding the bars with both hands as prisoners have as long as cells have been in existence.

"Is that necessary, Sheriff?" Sharon said crisply. "You're treating him as if he were a criminal or something. You've known him since he was born.

24

Surely his age –"

"Age ain't got nuthin to do with it, Miss Sharon, he's accused of murder. I have to treat him that way, got no choice. Besides, he's older than Billy the Kid, and look how many men he's killed."

He moved out into the office to again get comfortable at his desk. He moved his chair to the other side and left the door open where he could keep an eye on the trio. He grunted as he sat down, rocked the chair back on the back legs, and put his feet up on the desk.

Sam sank down on his cot, "I'm in such a mess."

He rested his head in his hands, looking down at the floor.

Sharon took the bars in both hands, "What happened?"

The haunted look returned to Sam's eyes as the scene again played across his mind. "I came home to find mama lying in a pool of blood. She said some drifter had tried to attack her, but she stabbed him with a paring knife. Guess he turned it around and used it on her."

Both girls began to cry. They knew his mother well.

"That is too horrible for words," Candace sobbed.

It was too much for him. Sam began to cry as well, his shoulders heaved with silent sobbing.

After a few minutes, Sharon got control of herself. "But why you? Why would they have you locked up?"

He held both hands up, then let them fall in consternation. "I was covered in her blood from holding her and was headed to the barn with the knife in my hand. I guess that wasn't too smart, but I never thought anybody was around, or how it'd look if they were. I just needed the knife to cut something to bury her in."

"Well surely the sheriff knows that you –"

Sam shrugged, "He said it don't matter what he thinks, I got to stand trial."

Both girls began to talk at once, reassuring him that the trial would only be a formality, that he had nothing to fear.

Nothing to fear, he thought, if only that were true.

<>

The sheriff shepherded the girls out the door, locked it behind him and headed off to the saloon to find the judge. He wasn't a drinking man himself, but he knew in small towns like Turkey Creek, the saloon was more than a place to get a drink, it was communications central. It was the only place large enough for people to meet, offered the only entertainment in town, often doubled as a courthouse and even housed the church on Sunday when there was someone to conduct services. It was a known thing that when men hit a town, it was the first place they'd go to find out what was going on.

The sheriff found the judge exactly as promised, asleep on the back porch of the saloon. "Aw, Judge, how come ever time I need you to be judicial you're wobble-kneed?"

He helped the old man to his feet.

The judge tried to focus on him. "I am most assuredly not wobble-kneed. From the position where I have spent the better part of the evening, that would require an improvement on my part."

He looked at the peace officer through incredibly bloodshot eyes.

"Did you tell those girls they could see Sam Duncan?" The sheriff maneuvered the magistrate into the back door of the saloon and motioned for the bartender to bring a couple of cups of coffee.

"Certainly. They asked if they could see him, and I am not one to stand in the way of the happiness of young people.

"I thought it odd, though. Why do you suppose they were asking me instead of their father? And two girls?

"Perhaps I spoke prematurely, a threesome is certainly not –"

The bartender came over to slide two chipped cups on the table then slopped coffee from the small blackened pot into them. He headed back to his position behind the bar, stopped as if having further thoughts on the subject, then turned and left the pot on the table.

Fancher shoved a cup of disgustingly thick coffee into the judge's hands. "Drink this, you old fool, they weren't asking your permission to court. I have him locked up in my jail; they were wanting to visit him."

"Humph," the judge said, "you should indeed have him locked up in your jail if he is trying to have relations with two young women at the same time. That's most unseemly."

"Concentrate, Judge," Fancher said as if he were talking to a two-year-old, "it has nothing to do with courting. He's locked up for killing his mother. You're going to have to have a trial."

"A trial?"

The judge drew himself up to his full height and

took the corner of his vest in his hand, "Can't you see, man, I'm in no shape to have a trial."

Fancher's head snapped back as the judge's pungent breath washed over him. He rose to support the little man, but stepped back to hold him at arm's length.

"I know that, you old fool, why do you think I'm trying to sober you up?"

"Is that what you are doing? Then why are you wasting my time with stories of courting and young people? We have serious business to conduct. We're going to need a lot more of this coffee.

Chapter 5

"You don't think he really did it, do you?" Sharon whispered in a conspiratorial tone.

"Sharon!" Shock distorted Candace's face. "How can you say that?"

"Humph." Sharon shrugged one shoulder at her friend, clearly unused to having someone question something she said. "People can do strange things, you know, in the heat of the moment."

"Why would he have a heated moment with his mother?" Candace returned to the task of pinning the dress to hem it as her friend stood on a footstool. "You know how close he and his mother were."

"Yes, I know, but life can be full of surprises."

Candace removed the pins from her mouth to speak. "Oh, you talk like some kind of sophisticated world traveler. You're no more a 'woman of the world' than I am."

Sharon put her hands on her hips and a haughty look came over her face. "Ha! You've never even been outside the county, but I on the other hand—"

"Have what? Have gone on a couple of trips with your father? Denver and Kansas City?"

The haughty look changed to anger. "Why you little –"

They stood face to face, glaring at one another. Then the look of anger melted from Candace's face,

"What are we doing?" she said softly.

"What?"

"We aren't mad at each other; we're just taking it out on one another. I didn't mean what I said."

Sharon enveloped her friend in a hug. "I didn't either. It's going to be all right. Sam is innocent, and the trial will show that."

◇

The judge sat sanitized cleaner than a fresh-licked newborn kitten. The saloon had undergone the magical transition to courtroom, which primarily meant the bar was closed, much to the consternation of the regular clients. Tables had been moved to the side except for one now used as the judge's bench and the two that would serve for the prosecution and the defense to sit behind. The chairs were arranged in rows and had been occupied as quickly as they had been put in position. It was standing room only, entertainment in town being rare as wild duck eggs.

Sober, the judge came much closer to looking the part. He had on his cleanest suit, had shaved the area separating his pork chop sideburns and walrus mustache and had on enough lilac water to draw bees from four counties.

Turkey Creek did have a lawyer in the person of Roger Eggleston. Forced to operate as the town barber by a lack of legal business, he had shunned his apron today for the opportunity to serve as the prosecutor. The county paid. Otherwise, had Sam the financial resources to offer a more lucrative stipend, Eggleston might have been serving as attorney for the defense.

He came in to take his place at one of the tables.

He had his lawyer suit on, long and lean with a drawn face that might better have suited an undertaker. He had his entire law library – Blackstone's Commentary – tucked under his arm. He carefully placed the tome in a prominent position on the table in full view of the entire courtroom.

The sheriff brought Sam in, removed the manacles, and seated him at the other table, taking the chair next to him.

Judge Larribee looked over at the lawyer, "Since you are not seated with the prisoner, I take it you are the prosecutor today?"

Eggleston rose, took his lapel in his left hand, struck a pose and said, "I am, Your Honor, duly appointed by the county judge."

The judge looked at him distastefully, "Too bad, it would be a better trial if you were defending this young man." He pointed at Fancher with the handle of his gavel. "The sheriff could prosecute."

Fancher swallowed hard and looked as if he would rather be out of it.

Eggleston poked his nose in the air. "The defendant does not have sufficient resources to retain representation, Your Honor."

"I thought that might be the case."

The judge looked over at Sam, sitting alone at his table. "Well, as all of the legal talent in town is either here at the bench or over at the prosecutor's table, I don't suppose you have counsel?"

Sam looked puzzled. "Counsel?"

The judge looked mildly annoyed. "That means, do you have a lawyer?"

He wondered if he would ever get to preside over a trial where everything was done by the book, in the proper manner. His trials all seemed to be such makeshift affairs.

Sam's puzzled look intensified. "You just said there ain't any here, didn't you?"

The judge banged his gavel. "I know that! I have to ask you for the record."

Sam shrugged. "Then, for the record, I don't have one."

The judge looked at the lady sitting next to him. "Write it down. Write it down."

"Don't you try to bully me, Horace Larribee, I don't have to do this, you know. The post office is closed while I'm over here, and I'm not really supposed to do that."

A big woman, Mrs. Broadie looked more than a match for the judge.

"Harrumph. Well, be that as it may…" He turned his attention back to the defendant. "Do you intend to defend yourself?"

"Do I have a choice?"

Larribee sneered. "That's, do I have a choice Your Honor?"

Sam looked downcast. "I don't know how to speak this lingo, and I don't know anybody that'll speak for me."

He frowned as he looked around the room. "This is starting to look a lot like a game that everybody knows how to play but me."

"You have a point," the judge nodded slightly, "so please allow me to tell you, the jury and the spectators assembled here a bit about frontier justice, lay out the ground rules, as it were."

"If everybody would talk English it'd help more than anything," Sam muttered.

The judge ignored the comment, sat forward in his chair where he could put both elbows on the desk and formed a steeple with his hands.

"You see, normally in a trial it is in very poor taste for the bench to say anything that might affect either side of a case."

Sam looked even more confused, "If the furniture is gonna start talking, the Sheriff getter lay hold on me because I'm out of here."

The judge looked at the ceiling. "'The bench' simply refers to the place where I sit. I'll be the one doing the talking."

"Then why didn't you say that? What are you blabbing about furniture talking for? I think you're just trying to confuse me even more."

The judge closed his eyes and sighed. "I'll do my best to talk so that even you can understand.

"As I was saying, the judge conducting the trial normally doesn't interfere in the presentation of the case much, but out west where experienced personnel often does not exist to adequately serve the needs of both the prosecution and defense, the bench often has to intercede on either or both sides to insure justice is done. I would say that is the situation here."

Larribee turned to look at the prosecutor, "You understand what I'm saying, Mr. Eggleston?"

"I do, Your Honor, we have had to do that on many occasions." He shrugged. "Actually, I suppose we have to do it all the time."

The judge pointed an accusing finger at the lanky lawyer. "Yes and when we do you've tried to use it as grounds for an appeal."

Eggleston looked at the judge over the top of his small wire-rim glasses. "As I shall probably do again if

I don't like the outcome."

Larribee raised his voice, "You're just trying to make me look bad before the next election."

The two ran against each other every year for the position of judge. Depending on the whims of the voters at any particular time, they had ended up taking turns being on both sides of the bench.

Eggleston snorted. "I don't have to try to make you look bad, you do well enough on your own."

The gavel slammed down. "One more remark like that, and I'll have you up for contempt of court."

Eggleston shut up. He'd done the same thing when he was up there on the bench, and he knew it. He had made his point and didn't want to overplay his hand.

Larribee forced his mind back to the business at hand.
"Where was I? Oh yes, Mr. Duncan, did you understand?"

"Not a word. Was that English you were speaking?"

"Ah, well, let me put it this way. You do the best you can, and the court will try and make sure your rights aren't trampled on. We will overlook your lack of knowledge of proper courtroom protocol."

Sam shook his head. "I still don't have the faintest idea of what you just said."

"You talk for yourself, and I'll try to keep you from making any mistakes."

Sam's mouth fell open. "That's what you said?"
"More or less."

Sam shook his head slowly. "I got a bad feeling about this, but I guess I got to eat what I find on my plate."

In spite of the encouragement of the girls, Sam

was not kidding himself about his chances. He calculated that a snowball had a better chance surviving in hell than his chances of coming out of this unscathed. Sam was a very practical young man.

They began to select a jury. Instead of challenging for cause as might have happened in the big city, it was more of a process of finding those who were sober enough to serve.

Chapter 6

The jury was selected and installed in the jury box, which consisted of the steps leading up to the second floor. They were clearly eager to get this over with and get the bar back open again.

The judge and prosecutor were not in that big a hurry. It was only during legal proceedings that they had the opportunity to be key players in the community and they both wanted it to last. They were also well aware that they were campaigning for the next election.

The judge looked over to Eggleston. "Counselor, do you have an opening statement?"

Eggleston walked to the front, struck his pose, this time holding both lapels, and eyed the jury with a piercing stare.

"Gentlemen of the jury," he projected in a voice intended to be heard all the way to the back row of the room, "the prosecution will prove beyond the shadow of a doubt that the defendant," he altered his pose to point an accusing finger at Sam, "willfully and in cold blood murdered his own mother and was in the middle of attempting to dispose of her body when the sheriff caught him in the act."

"Wait a minute," the sheriff rose to his feet.

Judge Larribee silenced him with a hand. "You'll have your chance on the stand, Sheriff. In the opening statement, each side gets to say how they see things. You know how this works; this is not the first case you've been involved in."

Fancher sat back down, "No, Your Honor."

Eggleston smiled as all eyes turned back to him. "Thank you, Your Honor. We believe the facts will support the charge of murder and believe the jury will have no trouble reaching that decision."

He walked back like a strutting bird and took his seat.

The judge looked at Sam. "Opening statement, Mr. Duncan?"

Sam gave him a blank look, "I don't know what you want me to do."

"You give the sort of talk that opposing counsel just gave."

Sam put his hand on his forehead making a gesture of resignation with his left hand. "I can't talk like that."

The judge had a pained look, as if he had just eaten something that disagreed with him. "Did you do it, Mr. Duncan?"

Sam straightened up; this was a question he could answer. "Of course I didn't!"

The judge leaned forward to peer at Sam. "You think the facts will prove that?"

"There were no witnesses that can back me up that I didn't, but I guess I can't see how anybody could prove I did it when that ain't true either. Reckon I'm just gonna have to trust that folks can see the truth of it."

Larribee leaned back and held up his hands. "That's called circumstantial evidence, Mr. Duncan. In the case that there are no witnesses, the jury will be weighing the circumstantial evidence trying to tell whether you did it or not."

Sam frowned. "Well I didn't and I can't see how any of this circumcised evidence can prove I did."

The judge snickered and then banged his gavel to silence the other laughter in the room. "Then that is your opening statement, Mr. Duncan. Mr. Prosecutor, call your first witness."

"Prosecution calls Sheriff Fancher."

The sheriff came forward, was sworn in and took his seat by the judge's table. He had dressed for the occasion with his cleanest shirt and a fresh boiled collar. He lowered himself into the seat with a grunt.

Eggleston closed in on him like a predator. "Sheriff, can you describe for us the events that transpired the day you rode in to the Duncan ranch?"

"I reckon so. I rode up just checking on things, since I was out that way. I'd already had my breakfast, but was thinking I might get a cup of coffee, maybe a stack of pancakes." He smiled. "Mrs. Duncan was a mighty fine cook."

Eggleston waved his comments aside. "Sheriff, your culinary habits were really not what I was trying to ascertain." The lawyer turned his attention to the bench. "Judge, could you ask the witness to be more responsive to the questions?"

The sheriff scowled at him, clearly not liking being called down in public.

The judge said, "Just answer the questions, Sheriff. No need to elaborate on things he doesn't ask you about."

"I thought people might want to know how come me to be out there."

He shifted in his chair and took a fresh run at it.

"Anyways, as I rode up, young Sam came out on the porch looking mighty dazed. When I got close I seen he had blood all over him and was holding a knife in his hand."

The sheriff leaned back and made a dismissive gesture with his hand. "Naturally, I throwed down on him. I mean, I've known him since he was a pup, but covered in blood and carrying a knife, I weren't taking no chances until I knew what was what, know what I mean?"

Eggleston came closer. "By 'throwed down', you mean you covered him with your weapon?"

Fancher's eyes narrowed. "Everybody knows what throwed down means. Of course I fetched out my gun. Dang eastern lawyers."

"I just have to have it clear for the record. Go on, Sheriff."

Sheriff Fancher eyed the lawyer as if he were considering putting some well-placed knots all over his head and was measuring him for the location.

"Well, I had him toss his hardware and put the cuffs on while I could look things over."

"By the term hardware, you mean ..."

The sheriff slid forward in his chair, leaning out with a hand on one knee, the look he gave the lawyer was openly hostile. "The gun and the knife; don't you speak English?"

"Don't lose your temper, Sheriff, I just have to make sure –"

The sheriff interrupted again, scooting forward in his chair, "Yeah, I know, just for the record. If you aren't careful, I'm going to take that record and put it somewhere that'll make you walk bowlegged for a week."

"Sheriff!" The judge banged his gavel.

"Well, he's rawhiding me."

The sheriff sat back in his chair, emphasizing his point with a flamboyant gesture in the air. "I ain't gonna stand for it."

Judge Larribee scowled at him. "How would you like to be locked in your own jail for contempt of court?"

"I got contempt for this court all right, and I'd like to see you try and lock me in my own jail. There wouldn't be a square foot of this whole town left standing before you got that done."

Larribee cleared his throat. "Let's calm down here. Just answer the questions."

Fancher jerked his thumb in the direction of the lawyer. "He better quit putting the spurs to me."

The color had drained out of Eggleston's face. The lawman might be putting on years and weight, but the lawyer was under no illusions as to what would happen if the man decided to come at him. "Sheriff, just tell us what you found after you got him chained to the porch rail."

That diverted the Sheriff's attention, and he, too, looked a little uncomfortable as he thought back to frame an answer. "Carved up like a side of beef, she was. I hope to God I never have to see something like that again."

Eggleston got as close as he dared. "Were the wounds caused by the knife Duncan had in his hand?"

The color returned to Fancher's face in a rush. "Well, how on earth would I know that? A knife is a knife."

"Were there any other bloody knives lying around?"

"No."

Eggleston turned and took a couple of steps toward the jury, wanting them to particularly hear what he had to say a little slower now, "Then it is reasonable to assume the bloody knife he had in his hand was the one used?"

Fancher nodded. "Unless the man carried it off with him."

Eggleston spun back to face the sheriff and raised his eyebrows in surprise, "Man?"

"Well, Sam said there was this drifter that–"

The lawyer closed on the sheriff. "You have knowledge of another party at the scene?"

"Sure, Sam said –"

The lawyer cut him off, "I mean personal knowledge."

"Well, no, but Sam is –"

Eggleston quickly turned to the judge. "Your Honor, objection. Hearsay."

The sheriff's face flushed red. "You pencil-necked lawyer, you interrupt me one more time and–"

Eggleston backpedaled quickly, nearly going down.

"Sheriff!" the judge banged down his gavel. "Objection sustained."

The judge looked at the lawman. "Sheriff, this isn't your first trial, you know how things work."

The lawman focused an icy stare on the jurist. "I told you what was going to happen if he kept spurring me."

"He isn't spurring you. You don't have direct knowledge of some drifter in the area, do you?"

"No, but them living way out there like that and knowing Sam the way I do –"

"You know you can only testify to something you know first-hand. Sam will have to do his own testifying about this drifter."

Sheriff Fancher's voice became small and even. The menace in it was chillingly clear. "I'll tell you what I do know. I know people better quit cutting me off in mid-sentence. That ain't courtroom procedure; it's bad manners, and I ain't excluding judges from what's fixing to happen."

"Judge, I'm through with this witness." Eggleston struggled to compose himself, pulling on the collar that suddenly seemed very tight and clearing his throat as he returned to his seat.

"Your witness," the judge said to Sam. "You can ask him questions if you wish."

Sam stood and got right to the point. "Sheriff, you didn't actually see me do anything, did you?"

"Nope."

He came around the table and walked to where the sheriff was sitting next to the judge's table. "And the only reason you put them chains on me was because you didn't know what was going on?"

The sheriff nodded, "That's it."

"Sheriff, do you think I did it?"

Fancher shrugged. "No, I really don't. Wasn't sure for a while, but now I reckon I don't figure you for it."

Eggleston was on his feet. "Objection! Calls for a conclusion."

"Sustained." The judge banged down the gavel. "The jury will disregard."

One of the men held up his hand. "How do we unhear something we done already heard, Judge?"

"Just remember the Sheriff's opinion is not what counts here, only the facts."

"Sheriff, are you surprised that nobody seems to have seen this drifter my mother was talking about?"

The sheriff smiled. "For somebody that doesn't understand what's going on, you're asking some mighty sensible questions. No, I ain't surprised. Your place is so far out there, and if'n he done what you say he done, I reckon there's no way he would go where anybody would see him."

"But you are saying you believe such a drifter exists?"

Fancher scratched his head as he thought. "Well, the court has already made it that what I think don't stack up to much around here, and I can't prove that there is or ain't such a man. But I will give you this much, given the area of your place, such a man surely could exist."

Sam looked at the judge. "That's all the questions I can think of."

"All the questions I can think of, Your Honor."

"Ain't that what I said?"

"Oh, never mind, the witness may step down."

Chapter 7

Sharon leaned over to her friend. "Isn't this the most exciting thing you ever saw?"

The girls sat third-row-center in seats that were quickly given up when they walked up to them and glared at the occupants. Sharon was used to having her way, and her father's standing in the community very much backed that up.

Candace shook her head. "I don't think it's exciting, I think it's scary. I'm afraid for what might happen to Sam."

"Oh, poo, Sam will be all right. We know he didn't do what they are saying."

"We may know it," Candace gestured toward the stairs with her head, "but look at that so-called jury. They aren't half paying attention, they just keep looking over at the bar licking their lips. They aren't thinking about anything but the bar being closed. It doesn't seem to me as if it is going well at all."

Sharon scowled as the truth of that statement suddenly became clear to her. "Well why did they pick a bunch of bar dregs anyway?"

"They're all drinking friends of the judge."

Sharon started to stand. "That isn't right, I'm going to object."

Candace pulled her back down. "Shhhh. All you'll do is get us tossed out of here."

Sharon looked at her friend. "It isn't right, I tell you."

She pulled out of Candace's grasp and stood. In a loud voice she said, "I object!"

Startled, the judge looked over his glasses at her. "I beg your pardon?"

Sharon waved an accusing finger at him. "Judge, this is a farce."

Holding the gavel by the head he pointed right back at her.

"Young lady, you have no legal standing here, sit down before I have you removed from court."

"Humph! This isn't a court; it is a saloon, no matter what we might be pretending. Nonetheless, someone needs to say something. Your so-called jury is made up of men that daddy won't even use for day work because they are undependable drunks."

Larribee banged his gavel. "That'll do, young lady. Sheriff, remove her from the courtroom."

Fancher leaned his chair back on its two back legs. "For what? For telling the truth?" He made no move toward her.

The judge half-rose from his chair shouting at the big man. "Sheriff, I'm directing you to remove her!"

Fancher set the chair down hard, stood and looked over the group. "I'll tell you what, Judge. I'll throw out any three men of your choice, all at once if you want, but I ain't laying hands on that little spitfire."

Larribee pointed his gavel at three men as he named them. "Payton, Silsbee, Tucker, get her out of here."

The three advanced on Sharon. A parasol came out from under her seat and a look came into her eye that should have been adequate warning.

It wasn't.

The three ducked their heads, hunched their shoulders and reached for her. Blows rained down on their heads. Payton almost succeeded in pinning her arms from the back. The brightest smile in town clamped down on his wrist, drawing blood.

He staggered back, yowling and holding his wound. This freed her to use well-manicured fingernails on Tucker's face. In his haste to escape the clawing, he fell over the front chairs, recently vacated by men dodging to keep from catching an errant blow from the parasol. He crawled franticly away.

Silsbee was just about to bring the barrel of his pistol down on her head when he heard the ratchet of the hammer being pulled back on the sheriff's pistol. "I'd rethink that, was I you," Fancher said.

Silsbee backed away, hands held high.

Fancher released the hammer on his Colt and slid it back into the holster. "Looks like you're going to have to do it yourself, Judge."

"Young lady!"

Sharon looked down at the parasol, now bent at a strange angle. She smoothed her skirt and patted a few errant curls back into place as she gained her decorum. "All right, all right, I'm sitting down, but this isn't right."

She straightened and re-pinned her hat, maintaining eye contact with the judge. Just before she resumed her seat she said, "Daddy put you in that job, and I intend to see that he corrects that error."

The judge paled. Her father was the big he-bull in these parts and there was significant danger that he would listen to her. Still, the judge had always done exactly what Colonel Delmar wanted him to do, and he thought – no, he hoped – his position was safe. She was, after all, just a young girl. He gave her one more glance.

But a really tough young girl, he conceded.

<><

It was after dark when Rafe Logan rode into Millers Run. His neck hurt as if it were on fire. He wanted a drink in the worst way, but he didn't want too many people getting a good look at him here.

He made his way over to the livery stable. Inside the barn, an old man alternated tossing hay to the animals and pulling on a jug.

"Perfect," Logan said under his breath. "He won't remember much tomorrow."

He pulled his hat down where it would shade his face from the faint lantern light. "While you're tossing hay, you mind throwing some in a stall for this horse? And maybe a little extra I can bed down on?"

The old man ducked his head trying to see under Logan's hat, but he couldn't make out much.

"Sure thing, stranger, that'll be two bits, in advance."

Logan fished out the coins. "I got a silver dollar to go with it if you've got another one of them jugs."

The old man reached for the money with a grimy hand. "I think that can be arranged."

The transaction concluded, the old man grabbed his hat and scurried out the door.

On his way to the saloon or maybe a restaurant, Logan thought.

He spread his blanket over the scratchy hay and

settled down on it. A bed would feel better, but he couldn't chance the exposure. This will have to do. At least it's fresh hay, smells good.

He wet the corner of his bandana with the liquor and began to dab at his neck. The alcohol sent pain raging through his body to the point that his muscles locked up and he couldn't breathe. He exhaled a couple of times trying to catch his breath.

When he could breathe again he swore to himself softly then said, "Stupid woman. I wish I could go kill her all over again for doing this to me."

Logan got to his feet and found a sack of grain. He poured some out in a tin plate and used his gun butt to grind it up. He added water and whiskey and continued to work it until he made a paste he could use as a poultice for his wound.

He continued to pull on the jug as he rummaged around until he found what looked like the old man's only clean shirt and tore the tail off it to make a bandage. He put the rest of the shirt in his saddlebag for future applications.

He gave a half grin that looked more like a sneer. "That old fool is never going to figure out what he did with this shirt."

His side shook with silent laughter. "And the shape he's about to be in he'll be dead sure he did it."

Logan tied the bandage in place with the ground-meal poultice up against the wound. The pain again made him wobble-kneed and he dropped heavily back in his nest of hay.

He went back to work on the jug again, muttering under his breath, "Yeah, wish I could kill her all over again."

Chapter 8

Sam looked at the jury and came to the same conclusion the girls had. He knew this wasn't going well and wondered what he could do to get their attention.

"Present your next witness," the judge said to the prosecuting attorney.

"Prosecution calls Sam Duncan."

"You can't do that." The judge again banged his gavel. "He'll be a defense witness if he's a witness at all. A man can't be forced to testify against himself."

Eggleston looked down his nose at the judge. "You think I don't know that? I'm the only one here that's actually been to law school."

He had been looking for an opportunity to get that campaign jibe in where the voters would hear it. He turned and smiled at them, sure he had scored a major point.

"You better watch your mouth, Counselor; I know I can get you locked up for contempt. And I don't think anybody here is impressed by a mail-order law school, a half dozen mail-order lessons and an old, used law book."

The judge was still stinging over the realization that he probably didn't have the power to get that contempt order accomplished when he threatened the sheriff, and wasn't entirely sure the sheriff would lock up Eggleston. He decided he didn't want to take the chance of trying and failing. But one thing was for sure, he didn't intend to sit still and let the lawyer upstage him on the election.

Eggleston sounded indignant, "For your information that law school was –"

Bang! The gavel slammed down again. "We aren't here to discuss your so called legal education. I was about to rule on whether you could call Duncan as a prosecution witness."

"It's all right with me, Judge," Sam spoke up. "One way or the other, I have to get up there and tell my story."

The judge looked annoyed. "Very well, but while you are on the stand, I will handle from the bench any defense cross examination that is necessary."

Eggleston jumped to his feet. "Objection, Judge!"

"Noted, but I've already explained about that. If we had another barber in town, maybe it wouldn't be necessary." His voice dripped with sarcasm.

The lawyer scowled at the intentional slight and folded his arms while Sam took the stand and was sworn in. Eggleston advanced on him like a cat stalking a cricket.

"Mr. Duncan, will you recount for us the events as you recall them?"

Sam dreaded this. "Are you planning to interrupt me in the middle of every sentence like you did the sheriff?"

Eggleston folded his arms. "Probably . . . that's how it's done."

"Seems mighty rude to me." Sam composed himself. "I rode all night to get home from the roundup where I was working."

Eggleston quickly moved in front of Sam to confront him. "You rode at night? You expect us to believe you could do that?"

"There was a full moon, and I stuck to the roads, it wasn't hard. Anyways, when I got there, I found her all cut up. I took her head in my lap and she said that –
"

Eggleston's eyebrows rose. "Are you saying she was alive?"

"Yes." Sam nodded somberly. "She said she had been holding on to say goodbye."

The lawyer scoffed in an exaggerated manner for the benefit of the jury. "Oh come now, Mr. Duncan, and I'm sure she had the presence of mind to name her killer?"

"Yes. She said it was a drifter with a scar on his face leaving him with a marled eye. She said she gave him another scar with her paring knife before he took it away and used it on her."

"Ahhhhh." Eggleston held up one hand, finger pointing to the ceiling. "Did you get that, members of the jury, not one, but two scars. You would do better to keep your story to a believable level, Mr. Duncan."

Bang! The gavel sounded again. "Counselor, you are badgering the witness. You will save such remarks for your summation."

"Very well, Your Honor. We certainly want to do justice here."

He turned to survey the crowd. "Speaking of justice, almost everyone in town is here, if there is a witness who saw this mysterious stranger, the prosecution would very much like to get their testimony to support the contention of this young man. Anyone? Speak up if you saw him."

He looked around, waiting for someone to step forward, "No?"

He turned back to Sam. "I thought not."

"The sheriff said that –"

Eggleston cut him off. "The judge has already ruled on that. The sheriff's opinion or the opinion of anyone else is not germane here, only facts, only what someone absolutely knows to be true and can prove can be entered into evidence."

Something was going on here and Sam didn't get it. The judge and the lawyer both seemed to only care about upstaging each other; neither seemed to care about the trial either way, and he was caught in the middle. He didn't know any way he could change the ways things were going.

He felt absolutely helpless.

He said, "What I know to be absolutely true is I didn't kill my mother, and I believe her when she told me who did. I've always heard that people's last words were mighty powerful things."

Eggleston gave an exaggerated nod. "Oh, indeed they are. A dying declaration is one of the most powerful testimonies that can be given."

He got right in Sam's face. "If you can prove that she said it."

"She said it and she had no reason to lie."

"So all you have to do is prove it."

Sam looked down as he said softy, "You know I can't."

Eggleston looked at the crowd and gestured as if Sam had just convicted himself out of his own mouth. "I turn the witness over to the defense."

The judge rubbed his chin. "I can't think of anything that hasn't been covered. You ready to do your summation?"

"I am indeed, Your Honor."

He looked at Sam. "The witness may step down."

Eggleston struck the pose again. "I laid out in my opening remarks what I intended to prove and I have done that. It is very common when there is a lack of witnesses to have a case built on circumstantial evidence and many a trial has been conducted in just that manner. The evidence here is very clear.

"While we still do not know what caused him to do it, I submit to you that Sam Duncan did kill his mother with malice aforethought and tried to cover it up by inventing this mysterious drifter. I put it to you that if indeed such a man existed, he could hardly pass through this area without somebody at least knowing he was here, whether they knew what he had done or not."

He moved over to stand in front of the jury. "He had the means to do it; he was caught holding the murder weapon. He had the opportunity; he was there alone with her. And while we don't know the motive, I believe I have proven the case beyond a reasonable doubt."

Eggleston sat back down, looking very pleased with himself.

"Mr. Duncan, your summation?"

"I'm guessing that means you want me to make the same kind of talk he just made?"

The judge nodded. "That is correct."

Sam walked over in front of the jury the way the prosecutor had done. "Most of you know me. You know I'm honest and easy-going. Some of you probably even know how close I was to my mother. There is no way I would ever do what they are saying I did.

"As to me making up that drifter, you know our place is one of the first places you hit riding into this country. I know he just rode in and after he done what he done he knew he couldn't show his face in town, so he turned around and rode back out. T'ain't odd to me that nobody seen him and it didn't seem odd to the sheriff either.

"I'm telling you I didn't do it and you only have their word that I did. I don't see how you can do anything but believe that I'm telling you the truth."

The judge looked at him. "That it?"

Sam nodded.

"Sheriff, take the jury out to consider the case."

Chapter 9

The jury went across the street to the general store to deliberate. As they walked in the door, one of them said, "Anybody know how we're supposed to go about this?"

A lay-about by the name of Morris Clayborn said, "I do. I've been on a jury before."

"So what do we do?"

"First, we got to elect a foreman, somebody to speak for us."

"Anybody else ever done this before?" Nobody answered. "Looks to me like you're elected."

You could almost see Clayborn swell with his new-found authority. He had never been in a position of any importance before. "Then we go over all of the evidence and decide whether we think he done it or not."

Another man looked at him and said, "We aren't going to go back over all that again, are we? I've heard about all of that I intend to listen to. And I'm getting powerful thirsty."

There was a chorus of voices agreeing with him. Clayborn worked to keep his disappointment from showing. It looked like his time in the spotlight was going to be far too brief.

"Very well, let's take a preliminary vote. All that think he is guilty hold up your hand."

Every hand went up, that is every hand but his own. He thought for a minute. He could vote not guilty and force some discussion, stretch out his time in the sun by a little. But he knew how many of them needed a drink, and he knew such a move would likely earn him some lumps on his head and a quick election for a new jury foreman. He sighed and held up his own hand to make it unanimous.

"That's it then, let's head back over."

<>

The girls came forward to keep Sam company as the jury deliberated over in the General store.

"This trial was a farce." Sharon's face had bloomed into a full pout.

"Sounds like you've already pronounced me guilty." Sam tried for a weak smile, but failed even that.

She put a hand on his arm. "Oh no, no, but they sure made it hard for you. I didn't think they were fair at all."

"You do think I'm innocent, don't you? You do believe me?"

Both girls became animated as they assured him they had no doubts of his innocence. Somehow it didn't help.

"Jury's coming back!" someone shouted.

"So soon?" Candace said.

Sam sighed. "No liquor over at your Pa's store, is there?"

"No."

He made a palms-up gesture with his hands then let them fall. "There you go."

The men filed in, but instead of taking seats on the stairs again, they merely stood beside them.

Judge Larribee said, "Have you reached a verdict?"

Clayborn said, "I'm the duly elected foreman of the jury, Judge."

"How nice for you. I repeat, have you reached a verdict?"

"We have, Your Honor."

"The prisoner will rise and face the jury."

Sam and the sheriff both got to their feet.

"We reckon he's guilty, Judge," Clayborn said.

"So say you all?"

The whole group nodded as one.

Sam let out the breath he didn't know he had been holding. The worst had happened. His eyes came up to focus on the judge. No, maybe not.

The jury broke for the bar. The judge stopped them with a repeated use of his gavel. "Hold on there, I'm not through. I still have to do the sentencing."

The men all backed up, clearly not happy about it.

The judge sat there for several minutes, rubbing his forehead as he thought. The grumbling in the room began to growl like a small animal in the underbrush.

Finally he decided. "Since this entire case is based on circumstantial evidence, and since the defendant is so young and all, I can't in good conscience hang him."

He changed from addressing the court to speaking directly to Sam. "So I hereby sentence you to life at hard labor in territorial prison. May God have mercy on your soul, because I don't think I'm doing you any favor at all ruling that way."

Sam's hand went to his throat without him willing

it to be there. He couldn't catch his breath. This couldn't be. The law couldn't convict an innocent man, that wasn't how things were supposed to work.

Behind him he could hear the girls crying and fought the impulse to join them. His life was over; life in Territorial Prison was still a death sentence, just not a very quick one.

◇

Logan awoke early and saddled his horse. He made his way over to the bank just as light began to show in the east, painting the sky crimson. As the bank teller opened the back door, Logan pulled up his bandana, stuck a gun in the man's ribs and followed him in. People wouldn't be expecting the bank to open for a good hour yet.

"Not again," the teller said. The lanky young man was crestfallen.

His attitude puzzled Logan. "This happened to you before?"

"Twice," the harried clerk admitted. "I've been thinking of quitting."

Logan laughed. "If I was you, I'' think on it hard. Not everybody is likely to be as good-natured as I am. That is, assuming you open that safe. It's going to get really nasty around here if you don't."

"It ain't my money." The teller knelt and fumbled with the dial. He had to go through the sequence twice before he got it open.

"Sorry," he said, "I'm nervous."

"I reckon getting robbed is something nobody ever gets very good at." Logan gestured with his pistol barrel. "Sit down over there."

The teller seemed relieved. "So you're going to tie me up instead of hitting me over the head with that gun or shooting me? I much prefer that option."

"I aim to please."

Logan took pegging strings and tied the teller's hands to the chair behind him. "Although I may clout you yet if you go to making a bunch of noise."

"If it'll keep me from getting hit over the head, I shall be quiet as a mouse."

Logan went to the front window and peeked out around the curtain. He saw no signs of life, no one out on the street. Still, if an ambush were being planned, it would look exactly the same way. He knew firsthand about that from his days riding with a gang down on the border, and he had a scar on his lower back to prove it.

Scars, he had a lot of them. There were times that the pain and trouble involved getting so called 'easy money' made him wish he'd just stayed on the family farm and tilled the ground. But when he had that thought it passed quickly as he remembered eating dust behind a mule and the sweat, strain and sore muscles that went along with it. Maybe there was no such thing as 'easy money' but there sure was such a thing as gut-wrenching hard-earned money.

The teller tried to further set his mind at ease. "Besides, there's no point in my making noise anyway. No one lives close enough to hear and most are occupied with their breakfast. I calculate you have an hour to an hour and a half before Mr. Snodgrass condescends to come in, maybe more.

"He's the president of the bank, and he takes his own sweet time. Then too, even when they do see there's been a robbery, it'll take a bit of time to get the posse together as well. That ought to give you a nice jump on things."

"You really are very experienced at this."

The teller nodded. "You could say that."

Logan left by the back door, mounted and rode quietly out of town. It had gone well. No one had gotten a good look at him and the robbery had been uneventful. His luck seemed to be taking a turn for the better.

It was about time he caught a break.

<>

"I'm sorry, boy."

The sheriff's concern seemed to be genuine as he put the manacles back on Sam. "I don't really think anybody around here is thinking of appealing that sentence with a rope verdict still a possibility if it goes badly, but your mama was mighty well liked too.

"That might tempt somebody to bust you out of that hoosegow over there. I think I'll go ahead right now and take you to the county seat where that there prison wagon can pick you up."

The Greener shotgun cradled in the crock of the sheriff's arm may have discouraged any who had such thoughts or it may have just been the fact that it was a very dry trial and everybody was bellied up to the bar. Whatever the reason, they made the walk to the stable without incident, saddled mounts, and rode out of town the back way.

Sam looked over at the lawman as they rode. "I gotta know, Sheriff, did you mean it when you said you didn't figure me to be guilty?"

The sheriff seemed to be weighing his answer. "I

reckon you see by now that it's clear what I think is no never-mind, boy, but if it'll set your mind at ease, I don't think you killed your ma. I know you set store by her and I've thought on it a lot. I reckon I just can't see you ever hurting her."

"That means a lot to me, Sheriff. It don't change nuthin, but it means a lot."

They rode for several hours before they decided to stop and eat at a small lake. They made a meal out of coffee, skillet cakes and fatback and sat back to relax. Fancher leaned back against his saddle and let out a belch that came all the way up from his toes.

"It don't get much better than this, Sam, the sun warm on your face, out away from the hustle and bustle, full of grub with that little lake calling to you to wet a line."

"Reckon I'd have to agree if we was camping out instead of you taking me to prison."

"Sorry, that was kinda insensitive of me. I have to tell you I've been thinking on things, and that weren't no kind of trial at all. I figure that jury railroaded you sure as the sun is gonna come up tomorrow."

"What was your first clue? Them sitting over there licking their lips and staring at the bar instead of paying attention?"

"You called it there all right. If there was a bar dreg in town that wasn't sitting on that jury I don't know who it was."

Sam leaned his head back and stared up at the sky. "I never did figure out what was going on. It was like people were talking a foreign language."

"I could tell you was feeling that way. It just ain't right."

"Might not be right, but it's done."

61

"It galls me." The anger building inside of Fancher showed clearly in his face. "I put this badge on to serve justice, and generally I'd say justice wasn't up to me but to a jury, but –"

"But that wasn't much of a jury?"

"You called it." Fancher got up and went to the fire to get a cup of coffee. He stared absentmindedly at the pot, turned and walked back to where he had been sitting, stared at that a while, then continued to pace the camp, muttering to himself. The only phrase Sam caught clearly was, "It ain't right."

Sam knew it was gnawing at the lawman and figured the best thing to do was keep quiet and let him think.

In mid-pace, Fancher suddenly slammed his hat to the ground and yelled, "Dag-nab-it! I just can't swaller it and make it go down."

He turned to look at Sam. "Maybe it ain't the proper thing to do, but I'm going to give you a chance. No, I got to give you a chance. I couldn't live with myself if I didn't."

"I don't understand."

"It ain't hard to figure, I'm going to let you make a break. I've got me some fishing line in my saddlebag and I fancy trying that lake on for size. Come morning, I figure on using a rough rock to scrape up my forehead like you hit me with something, and when I get back I'll tell them you escaped on me."

Sam couldn't believe his ears. Was Fancher serious? Would he be shot in the back as he tried to escape? He looked at Fancher's face and saw nothing there but sincerity.

"Why you doing this, Sheriff?"

Fancher sat back down, seemingly at peace now

that he had made up his mind. He sat there for a few moments staring into the fire. Finally he said, "It's this badge, Sam. It stands for law and justice. What they done to you may have been within the law, but it had nothing to do with justice."

"I don't know how to thank you."

Fancher warded off the comment with one hand, "It ain't as much as you think. You'll be out of my jurisdiction, so soon as I get back, some Texas Ranger is going to come after you like a mad hornet. I figure you got two choices, race them for the border, or try to find this drifter and clear your name before they catch up to you."

"It'll have to be the second one, Sheriff. I promised Mama I wouldn't go after him when she begged me to let the law do it. That didn't work out too well, so I reckon now it's up to me to find him."

Fancher nodded. "Can't see how I'd do it any different were I in your shoes."

He looked up at the sky. "Be dark soon, you did say at the trial that you could ride at night pretty well?"

Chapter 10

It took the Millers Run banker, Filbert Snodgrass, two hours to come in and find his teller trussed up. It took another hour to raise a posse and set out. They cut the robber's tracks outside of town, but hit the county line long before they even got close.

The posse pulled up, and Marshal Frank Slade said, "This is as far as I can go."

Snodgrass was incensed. "You mean to say we can't chase them past the county line?"

Slade sat his horse on the ridge looking across the valley below. No dust cloud, or any sign of life was in sight.

"I'm a town marshal, Filbert, I ain't even supposed to chase him this far. It'd be different if we were hot on his heels. If I still had him in sight, we could legally chase him till we ran the shoes off our horses, but that ain't how it is."

The banker's face was so red, he looked as if he was about to explode. "Why don't we just post a flyer that says 'Come to Millers Run Texas – you can rob our bank and we won't even bother to chase you'?"

The marshal pulled a plug of tobacco from his vest and bit off a substantial chunk. Obviously the ride back was to be leisurely. "You get it printed, and I can get it posted."

The banker was red-faced again. "I was being

facetious, you idiot."

Slade's eyes locked on the banker, hard and unyielding. "I don't know what that word means, but I know what idiot means, it means I'm about to slap you off that horse."

Slade held the banker pinned by his glare, unblinking. Finally, Snodgrass looked down, small beads of sweat on his forehead, "Facetious means I was just kidding," he said in a small voice.

"You best have been kidding about that other word, too."

Slade replaced the plug of tobacco in his vest.

"Of course I didn't mean that. I was merely speaking in the heat of the moment." The banker wiped his neck and forehead. It wasn't that hot. "It was just my frustration showing."

"If I was feeling bad about breaking off the chase, it ain't bothering me no more."

The lawman swung his horse and led the posse back toward town.

The little man spurred his horse to catch up. "Wait, you men! I'd pay to have you come with me and catch him."

They stopped. One man said, "Pay? How much?"

"Five dollars a day."

The man busied himself cutting a chaw from a plug of tobacco. "Your teller said he looked mighty salty." Holding what he had cut between his thumb and forefinger he used it as a pointer to underline his thought. "A man don't get scars all over him like that by teaching Sunday school."

The banker didn't get it. "Surely you aren't afraid."

The man casually tucked the chew into the corner

of his mouth. His eyes narrowed as he responded, "You calling me yellow?"

"Why is everybody so touchy today? I just meant you didn't measure up to be a man that would be afraid of him."

The man spit and replaced the plug in his pocket before he turned his horse to go. "I ain't, but I figure five dollars ain't worth getting shot up over."

The rest of the posse turned and rode to catch up with the marshal, leaving the banker sitting alone, sputtering like a lantern about to blow out.

<>

Sam was hungry. He had ridden through the night and put on a lot of miles, but he had no money on him, and it was going to be mighty hard to run without any. As he rode, he considered the fact that the sheriff was unlikely to raise a posse and calculated he'd have at least two or three days before anybody was likely to be after him. He knew he had to have money to run. He pulled up on top of a ridge to see a little hardscrabble ranch down below him.

It'd have to do. He rode toward the house, small and square, but whitewashed and tightly built as was the small barn. As he came into the yard, a man came through the door of the barn, wet with perspiration. The man pulled a red bandanna from his pocket and began to mop his face and neck.

Sam reined in and smiled, "Lemme guess, tossing hay?"

The man smiled back. "You called it."

"I'm looking for work; I could help you with that."

"I got a hired hand; reckon that's all I can afford.

If you're riding the grub line I can stake you to a meal, though."

Sam shook his head. "I'm not looking for permanent work, got someplace to be. Thought you might have a little day work. Wouldn't object to a meal, though."

"You wouldn't object to this meal. My missus don't have to take a back seat to nobody when it comes to putting food on the table. There's some fried chicken and mashed taters sitting on the back of the stove."

Sam stepped down. "I'd say you just flung a craving on me. Man would have to be crazy to turn down an offer like that, but I gotta cut you some wood for the wood box or do something useful for you in return. It ain't in me to just take a handout."

"We'll see. Your horse looks a little used. Why don't you put him in the barn, and there's some grain in that bin to the left of the door."

"I'm beholden."

Sam stripped the saddle and turned the little bay into a stall. He poured a couple of scoops of grain into the trough. "Looks like we're both gonna get us a good meal."

As he approached the house, the man didn't wait for him to knock but yelled for him to come on in. A pleasantly plump lady with graying hair and a flowered apron put a plate overflowing with food on the table, then filled a coffee cup to the brim.

He whipped the hat from his head as if it were afire as she set down the plate. "I'm mighty grateful, Ma'am. My name is Sam Duncan."

"Sit down, young man; we don't stand on ceremony here. My name is Hattie."

She turned back to the stove, stopped, then added, "Did this old fool introduce himself?"

The man smiled a gentle smile. It didn't take a genius to see how the two felt about each other.

"It generally ain't a good idea out here to initiate introductions lessen the other party starts it, but I reckon I'd rather not be known as the old fool. My handle is Jeremiah Whittaker, but everybody calls me Pop."

Sam jumped up and took a couple of quick steps to shake his hand.

"Now sit yourself back down like Hattie said and tie on some of that fried chicken. She cooks it up so good that most of them yard-birds are volunteering to get into the house to take their turn in the pot."

"You silly man" Hattie laughed and swatted him with the dish-towel she was holding. She went back to fussing around the kitchen doing the incomprehensible tasks that women seemed to always find to do and men never seemed to understand.

"I been thinking on it, Sam," the little man said. "Homer, that's my hired hand, is off bringing in a little new stock for me. With him gone, I might have a couple of days' work, but it'd be back-breaking, gut-wrenching work. You probably wouldn't want to do it."

He pulled a pipe from his pocket and began to pack it with rough cut giving Sam time to think on it.

The only time Sam needed was for a big swallow to clear his mouth the way he'd been taught. "I ain't no stranger to hard work."

"I figured. I felt the calluses on that handshake. I got a corral out there about to fall down and like I said, have a hand off bringing in some fresh stock. I'll tell you the truth, I ain't got it in me to set posts no more, and I can't wait for Homer to get back to fix it up. It's gotta be ready by the time that stock arrives."

Sam nodded and paused with a fork full of potatoes half way to his mouth. "As long as we're telling the truth, I got me a little frustration riding me like a sore-backed horse. I could probably work a bunch of it out on a patch of hard ground like this."

Pop sent a cloud of smoke toward the ceiling. "Reckon you're right about that, this ground is so hard that even gophers hire out their digging."

"I figured," Sam said around another mouthful of food.

"You didn't ask what it paid."

"It'll be fair. Besides, I figure it'll give me the chance to put my boots under this table another time or two, and that's something that would sure enough pleasure me."

Chapter 11

Zeke Flagg rushed into the store to find the storekeeper putting air-tights of food on the shelf and Sharon and Candace having a little tea party in the chairs around the pot-bellied stove. It was too warm for the stove to be lit, but it was still the centerpiece of the conversation area.

Ray looked up, "Hello Zeke, kinda early for you to be out and about, isn't it?"

"I am the bearer of news."

"I see." Ray prepared to negotiate for the release of the information. "But I'm sure you need to get your shopping out of the way first?"

"I am a bit short on beans, and I fear that bacon went far too quickly."

Ray sat the items on the counter and waited expectantly. Flagg had both of the girls' full attention too.

With no preamble Flagg said, "Sam Duncan has escaped!"

"What?" all three said as one. "How? When?"

"You know the sheriff was transporting him, but he knocked him out and made a run for it."

"You don't say." Ray pushed the items toward him, adding a small sack of tobacco without even being asked. A tip for more important news than expected. Sometimes an item was taken back off the counter if the little man failed to produce news worth the value requested. This time it was more, and a nonverbal request for more detail.

Candace put it into words. "Sam wasn't hurt?"

"No, I guess he caught the sheriff by surprise."

Ray looked puzzled. "Wouldn't think Bill to be a man easily taken by surprise."

Flagg gathered up his bounty. "Nor would I."

"He didn't take out after him?"

"Said his head hurt too much to ride. Said he had a hard time even getting back, much less chasing a man."

"That doesn't sound much like him either," the storekeeper said.

"You'd have to take that up with him." Flagg turned and rushed out, eager to get on with his business.

The girls returned to their seats. Candace said, "I'm worried about him."

"You are such a mouse," Sharon laughed. "I find it exciting. I didn't know he had it in him."

"I suppose such a daring venture moved him up on your list of suitable men?"

Sharon raised one shoulder and moved her chin in line with it.

"Maybe. The selection in this two bit town is rather limited."

That's all they are to you, Candace thought, a selection, stock on the shelf like the items here in Daddy's store. Do you really think of them as people? Do you really care about any of them? You're like a bee flying from flower to flower. No, that's not right personifying cowboys as flowers. She smiled as she thought, could there be such a thing as a flower flying from bee to bee?

Sharon saw the small smile and said "If it's so serious, what are you smiling about?"

"Just something I thought about. It's not important."

But her mind was still on her friend no matter what she said. Candace was used to Sharon taking any man she herself might show interest in. Sometimes she thought it was intentional, Sharon's way of putting her in her place. Sharon could have any man she wanted. Still, she couldn't help but like Sharon, they had grown up together, and it had always been that way. It was just how things worked.

"It is serious, and I'm still worried about him."

◇

Sergeant William Jacob Stoker rode slowly into Turkey Creek. He'd gotten the telegram down the line and wasted no time getting on the trail. He always saw to it that Ranger Headquarters knew where he was and he always checked with Western Union when he hit a town.

The big ranger had collar-length black hair and a full, flowing mustache on top of skin tanned to leather by the sun. It all added up to a dark, menacing look that he fully lived up to. He wore a big Walker Colt on his left side in a cross-draw position that would be easy access standing, sitting or riding.

The sheriff came out on the board walk as the ranger rode up. "Howdy, Jake," he said, "figured you'd be coming."

He stepped off the boardwalk and extended a hand. They exchanged a perfunctory shake.

Stoker seldom showed any facial emotion. "It's my job. Telegram said something about an escaped prisoner?" He gave Fancher an appraising look. "Ain't like you to lose a prisoner."

Fancher got a sour look on his face. "You et? I'd kinda like to jaw with you a little before the wolves come in howling."

"I could eat. I reckon the judge that sent this telegram can wait. I'm kinda curious why it was him instead of you that sent for me."

Fancher steered the ranger over to the Bulls Head restaurant. The last thing he wanted to do was take him to the China Palace Saloon where he knew the judge was holding forth on the ineptitude of law enforcement, the affront to the law that an escaped prisoner represented, and how one of the most feared rangers in the state was wearing out horses coming to set things right.

The waitress put a steak big enough to ride in front of the ranger with a baked potato resting right in the middle of it since the steak took up the entire plate. Stoker went to work on it in a very businesslike manner, carving off a big bite and shoving it in his mouth.

Fancher eased into the subject. "I'm thinking things may not exactly be the way you're fixing to hear 'em when you talk to the people across the street."

"That so?" Stoker said around a jaw full of meat. "Why don't you tell me how you see things?"

Fancher pushed back in his chair, tipping his hat to the back of his head with a forefinger. "I think we got a drunk of a judge that railroaded a young man."

Stoker sawed off another man-sized chunk of the

meat. "You figure this Duncan to be innocent?"

"My gut tells me he is, but I can't prove it. I don't figure they proved it the other way either, though."

"Frontier justice can be that way."

Stoker washed down another big bite with a swallow of coffee. "You thinking I shouldn't be after him?"

"No, he was tried and convicted. Just wanted you to have an open mind and not be too quick on the trigger. And if you run across a man with a marled eye and a fresh scar on his neck, you might want to ask him some pointed questions."

"That what Duncan said?"

"That's what he said his ma told him before she died."

"A deathbed declaration is a mighty powerful thing. But since he got convicted, I'm guessing you only have his word that's what it was though, right?"

"That's right, but the boy has always been straight up with me, Jake. Just keep an open mind, that's all I'm asking."

"I generally try to do that." Stoker shoved another big bite in his mouth then gave Fancher a very direct look as he chewed. He swallowed and said, "Although it can be useful to know just what I'm supposed to be keeping an open mind about."

<>

Idiot sticks, that's what most working hands called posthole diggers. A foreman crossing the yard with a pair of them in his hands could empty a bunkhouse. Right now Sam was wielding them as if he were using them on the mysterious stranger instead of on the rock-hard ground.

Pop came over to pour a bucket of water into the hole. "I did tell you that you don't have to get all these poles set in a single day, didn't I? I ain't never seen anybody work as hard as you do."

Sam waited for the water to soak in and accepted the dipper of water the old man had held back from the bucket. "I ain't much on sitting around when there's work to be done."

"I wasn't kidding when I said I couldn't afford more than one ranch hand, but you've got me thinking I might have the wrong one."

"Thank you. That'd be mighty inviting if I was free to settle down. Right now I ain't."

He replaced the dipper and went back to pounding the earth with the diggers.

Pop decided to float a trial balloon. "I reckon you've got something stuck in your craw. If'n you get where you want to talk about it, Hattie says I'm a right good listener. If you don't want to, I won't be prying. Just wanted you to know I'm here if it suits you to talk."

Sam mumbled his thanks, then went back to work on the face of the mysterious stranger that he pictured in the dirt at his feet.

A short time later Pop came back with another bucketful of water to pour in the hole and another dipper for Sam.

"Man can dry out if he don't keep drinking water in this heat," Pop said, "especially working hard as you are."

"Won't argue with you there."

Sam drank it right down, then poured the rest of it over his head.

Pop shook his head slowly. "I'm starting to worry about your health . . . and your sanity."

"Health is fine," Sam grinned as he added, "not so sure about my sanity."

He stood and looked at the old man for a minute. Funny how you can know someone for such a short period of time and feel like you've known them all your life.

He decided the old man was entitled to know what trouble he had under his roof. "I got trouble riding my back trail."

Pop sat on the end of the wagon Sam was working out of and filled his pipe as he listened. "Figured as much. You finally getting around to telling me about it?"

Sam leaned on the posthole diggers. "I guess you deserve to know, I don't want to bring trouble down on you two. You've been real good to me."

Pop stuck the pipe in the corner of his mouth and set a match to it. "Somebody want a man bad enough to chase him, he's wearing a badge or looking to deliver a load of bullets."

Sam shrugged. "This ain't that clear. I think there's a badge involved, but it was another badge that set me loose, let me escape."

"Ain't that a caution? I reckon you got to tell me the whole thing."

"Why don't we go over to the house? Miss Hattie ought to know what a varmint she's got under her roof."

It was a two-cup of coffee story, and the pair listened attentively. When he finished, Hattie spoke first. "Why that wasn't fair. I can see this boy would never hurt his mother, what were those people thinking?"

Pop nodded. "Sounds like a pretty raw deal, all right. You don't worry none about bringing down trouble on us. You're welcome here as long as you want. We could keep you hid out if anybody come looking."

"Secrets don't keep, Pop. It'd come out, and then you'd be in the soup along with me. Besides, I couldn't live with this hanging over my head. The only chance I got at a life is to find the man with the scar."

"You could at least hide out here till things cooled off."

"I couldn't do that. I figure I've got a couple more days at best before some Texas Ranger comes boiling in here after me."

"Texas Ranger, eh? You best hope they don't send Jake Stoker. Once he gets on a trail —"

Chapter 12

Judge Larribee tried to appear very officious, but he was well into his day's recreational drinking and his efforts fell short.

"Ranger..." He hiccupped, paused with his hands to his lips as it passed, then continued. "I appreciate you reporting so promptly. We will expect the outlaw to be returned forthwith for transportation to territorial prison."

Stoker restrained his amusement at the little man. "I don't know about forthwith, but when I go after a man I get him."

"I've heard that about you. You don't want to take any chances either, he's a bad one. Anyone who would do that to their own mother, there is no telling what they'd do."

"So I hear. Well, I'm sworn to uphold justice, whatever that might turn out to be."

"Why would you say it like that?"

"Like what?"

The judge stood on unsteady feet, working to maintain focus then decided he didn't know either and let it drop. He walked back over to the bar and pounded for the bartender's attention.

Fancher said, "Are you impressed?"

The ranger turned back to the lawman to nod slightly. "Let's just say you wanted open minded, and you got it."

Fancher walked Stoker back over to the livery stable to get his trail rig together.

On the way, Stoker said, "That a new Colt on your hip?"

"No, I've had it for many years." Fancher pulled the weapon and ran a hand over it lovingly. "But I do take good care of it as one should for an old friend. It's gotten me through some scrapes."

Stoker touched the butt of his own weapon. "I feel the same way about this Walker Colt. Seldom see one in the hands of anybody but a Texas Ranger or an Army officer. I've near lost it a couple of times."

Fancher slid the weapon back into its holster.

Stoker suddenly turned an appraising look on the lawman as his interest in the gun suddenly became clear. "Wonder why the boy didn't relieve you of that gun before he rode away, being as how you were knocked out? If he was chasing some mysterious man, looks like he'd have felt the need for one."

There was an awkward silence.

"Lemme put it this way," Stoker said slowly. "Just because I'm willing to keep an eye out for the truth doesn't mean I approve of you intentionally letting this boy escape."

"Who said I did that?"

"I know the difference between a rock scrape and a lump caused by getting knocked out."

Fancher started to frame a reply, but before he made it, Stoker spoke again. "I know that wagon." He nodded toward an empty wagon sitting down the street, horses tied off to the brake. "You find the owner of it, and you'll find a first-class Bible thumper."

Fancher looked puzzled. "Preacher?"

"Circuit rider. We've crossed trails a number of times.
Has a right pretty little wife that keeps him on the straight and narrow."

"I thought it was God that kept men on a straight path."

Stoker grinned an uncharacteristic grin. "I don't think God minds a little help. Man that has a good woman behind him is a mighty lucky man in my books."

A man came out of the stable leading a horse. "You looking for the owner of that wagon? He and a pretty little filly went off hunting the owner of the saloon to get permission to have services there tomorrow. Tomorrow is Sunday, ain't it? I lose track. Anyways, I think they intended to start looking over at the general store."

Stoker swung up into the saddle and pointed the animal out of town.

Fancher laughed. "The saloon is the only room large enough for that all right, but I'll go see if I can help them out."

Stoker nodded. "Good. I've got to get on the trail . . . and Sheriff?"

Fancher stopped and looked back as Stoker continued, "No matter what I find, you can believe I will bring him back."

<>

"Hi there, young lady, are you the proprietor of this establishment?"

Herbert Green wore the black frock coat and cleric

collar that marked him as a circuit-riding preacher. He hadn't always been that and had come by his conversion hard, very hard. In fact, before he did it for real, he was a con man using the disguise of a preacher to make him above suspicion while he was conducting his nefarious activities. But then he started actually believing what he was selling, and when he made the commitment, he made it heart and soul.

Candace smiled a dazzling smile. "My father is. May I help you?"

"You may. This is my wife Peggy. May we put a flyer announcing our camp meeting in your store window?"

"Of course." She held out a hand to Peggy. "My name is Candace, we are so very pleased you are here."

Peggy returned the smile. "Thank you. We are also seeking the owner of the saloon to get permission to put the meeting on there."

"He has done that in the past." Candace looked past Peggy's shoulder. "I believe I see the sheriff pointing him over in this direction now."

A bald-headed, be-speckled little man began to scurry in their direction. They moved out on the boardwalk to await him. "Howdy, Preacher," another voice said.

They looked to see Stoker riding toward them.

"Well hello, Jacob, good to see you again," Herbert said. "Jacob," he said to Candace, "a good Biblical name." Turning back to Stoker he said, "Your mother must have been a praying woman."

Stoker tipped his hat to Peggy and said, "Ma'am, good to see you again." To the preacher he said, "She was, and still is, though I fear I require far more of it than I should. I depend a lot on her standing with the Lord to help keep me safe."

Peggy acknowledged the gesture with a smile and a small inclination of her head and said, "I'm sure in your profession she does worry about you."

"You know this young lady?" Herbert gestured toward Candace.

The hat came off. "No, just got here."

"Miss Candace Bates, may I introduce Sergeant William Jacob Stoker?"

"My pleasure," Stoker said.

Candace did not look pleased, and it was not well disguised.

"Is something wrong?" Herbert asked.

She glared at Stoker, "I know why the ranger is here. He's here to hunt Sam."

Herbert looked puzzled. "I don't understand."

Stoker gave up one of his meager smiles. "I reckon you've walked into something and don't know it, Preacher." Stoker replaced his hat. "I take it you don't think Sam Duncan is guilty, Miss Bates?"

Her words were measured and hard. "I do not."

"There's a jury that seems to disagree with you, although I've had me a little talk with the sheriff and he seems to think the boy got a raw deal."

Her look softened a little. "Did you believe him?"

"Ain't up to me to believe or not, he was sentenced and I got to go get him."

The hard look returned to her eyes.

He added, "But if it'll ease your mind any, I promised the sheriff I'd keep an open mind about this mysterious stranger the boy said his ma talked about. If I find anything that'll help Duncan, I'll see it's known."

"That's not much."

"Yes, Ma'am, but it'll have to do."

Stoker touched the brim of his hat again and turned his horse. He pulled up, turned in the saddle and looked back to add, "I will make you this promise, I'll get him back here alive lessen he leaves me no choice at all."

"I'll hold you to that."

"You leaving?" Herbert said. "I thought you said you just got here?"

"You know how it is toting a badge, Preacher; somebody always seems to be getting away if you don't get after them."

"My problem is just the opposite, Jacob, the people I'm after are all lost and I very much want to make sure they are found."

"Here's hoping we both get our man, Preacher."

"Thank you, and perhaps we'll cross paths again on down the trail."

"We do seem to keep crossing paths, all right."

The ranger jerked his heels into the horse's flanks and left town at a trot.

"You looking for me, Preacher? My name is Tucker, I run the saloon. Lessen you're from one of those denominations that favor taking the fruit of the vine themselves, I gotta figure you're looking for a place to hold services."

"Yes, Mr. Tucker we do need to see you about . . . my goodness but you're scratched up, have you had a run in with a wildcat?"

"You could say that, Preacher, you could surely say that. A lady wildcat. Right in the middle of a courthouse, too."

Chapter 13

"I normally pay a day hand a buck or two a day and found, depending on how hard the work is." Pop scratched his chin. "Ain't never had anybody do two weeks' work in just a couple of days before."

Sam smiled. "Pop, whatever you think is fair. You've fed me so good I feel guilty taking money from you at all, only right now I'm really in need of it."

Pop held out a couple of five dollar gold pieces. "Don't be silly."

"This is too much. It's a week's wages or better."

"Who's running this place, me or you? Wish you weren't in such an all-fired hurry to run off."

Hattie came up beside him. "Yes, please stay. We can hide you until things cool down, then help you set things right."

"I can't tell you how much it means for you to be willing to do that, but I know what I have to do."

Sam stepped up into the saddle. Pop handed him up a flour sack. It was heavy. Sam looked inside. The bag was full of corn fritters and beef jerky . . . and a Navy colt.

"Reckon if you're set on doing this you better have a way of defending yourself," Pop said. "Sorry, I can't spare a long gun."

Sam stowed the sack in his saddlebags, then stuck

the pistol in his belt. "I'm beholden."

Pop put his hand on his leg and looked up at him as he added. "Son, if you get it done or if they quit looking, you'll remember the way back won't you?"

Sam offered his hand. "I'll remember."

They shook, looking into each other's eyes for what seemed to be a long time. Putting it off wasn't going to make it any easier. Sam turned his horse and headed out. How did a man find someone when he didn't know what he look like, didn't have a hint of a trail to follow and had to duck and hide himself every time he saw anybody?

He remembered the teacher in the little one-room schoolhouse talking about this Cheshire cat in a book she was reading. Something about a looking glass. The cat had said "if you don't know where you are going, then any road will get you there." Something like that. He smiled. The cat might be right.

If any road would work, this one led to the town of Millers Run. Sam didn't know if it would be safe to ride into a town but hoped that there hadn't been time for the word to get out. He didn't think the sheriff would put flyers out on him, so he hoped all his trouble was still behind him. But even if it was behind him, he had no doubt it was coming fast.

Millers Run was a half dozen rough-board buildings situated by a small stream that ran only a few inches deep. But even though it had little water in it now, at times when the snow melt in the mountains was heavy, it could run full to the banks. The dirt trail he was on led to a dirt street, then to a small bridge over the creek.

He could see a bank, saloon, hotel, general store and livery stable plus one other building with no identification. Behind the main street, some small houses that were clearly personal residences stood as if taking a back seat to the business enterprises. There was no sign of life except a yellow dog skulking down the main thoroughfare looking guilty from whatever he had just been up to.

Sam tied up to the hitching post in front of the saloon.

He walked through the swinging doors to find it empty except for a grizzled old man behind the bar. "Could I get a drink of water?" Sam asked.

"I don't sell water."

"All right, make it a beer, with a water chaser."

Sam put one of the gold pieces on the bar. The man picked it up, bit it, made change, then drew a mug of the barely cool liquid.

"Where is everybody?" Sam drank down the water, ignoring the foamy mug.

"Riding posse with the sheriff. The bank was robbed."

"No fooling?"

"No fooling."

The man looked at Sam with open suspicion. Sam understood.

He was sure the man was thinking he could be the one they were looking for, that he had just circled back.

"Ain't ya gonna drink that beer?"

"No, but if you give me another glass of water you can have it."

The man pulled the beer over in front of himself and poured Sam another glass of water. "Don't get many gold pieces," he said. "The bank had some."

That made it clear. "If that one came from the

bank, it was because Horace Whittaker got it from them. He used it to pay me for some day work."

"Anybody could say that."

"Would anybody know that his nickname is Pop, wife's name is Hattie, and he has a hired hand that's off trailing in some cows?"

"What's his name?"

"What's whose name?"

"The hired hand."

"I think Pop called him Homer."

"I guess you're all right. You just look kind of familiar, but I figure I don't know you."

Sam held out a hand. "Sam Duncan."

The man gave it a perfunctory shake, the question mark intensifying in his eyes. "Even the name sounds familiar, but I still know we ain't met."

"Is your name a secret?"

"Socks Donovan."

"Socks?"

"Trust me, you don't wanna know."

Sam drained the glass. "Guess I better get down to the store and get me a few possibles."

"Sanchez is out with the posse, but I reckon his wife can help you with whatever you need."

Donovan seemed to have quit wondering about Sam. Maybe it was the prospect of him enhancing the local economy a bit. "I got a rabbit stew on if you get hungry. It ought to be ready here in a bit. Sooner if you don't mind crisp taters."

Sam walked through the batwing doors, turned and headed down the walk toward the general store. He was almost past the marshal's office before the poster registered on him. He backed up.

It was his own face staring back at him, a line drawing, but recognizable. It read 'Wanted dead or alive – for murder – Sam Duncan'. It had been posted by Judge Larribee along with a $500 reward.

Sam smiled. The fact that it hadn't been posted by Sheriff Fancher as would normally be the case meant something to him. He pulled it down, folded it, and put it in his back pocket. Now he knew why the saloonkeeper thought his name and face were familiar.

How long would it take for Socks to put it together? He thought he had better get his business done quickly. He heard hooves pounding and turned to see the saloonkeeper riding out of town, spurring hard.

"Not even that long, I guess," he said under his breath.
He'd have to get out of town as quick as he could, depending on how far away the posse might be.

Mrs. Sanchez was a rotund, happy little woman, glad to see someone and apparently had not seen the poster. He bought a little food, a used holster for the Colt that would fit on his belt, and salivated over the new Winchester rifle they had on display. It was well out of his price range.

If he was really the kind of man they thought him to be he'd just shoot the woman and take it along with all the money in the store. He wasn't, but was disturbed the thought had even crossed his mind.

What is this doing to me?

He loaded his purchases and rode down to the bridge. He turned and took an angle to go into the stream downtown. He rode in the water for a hundred yards or so, then turned and came back. He dismounted. It was a tight fit getting the horse under the bridge, but he made it, then mounted and headed upstream, in the direction the saloonkeeper had ridden. It was a gamble, but it might work.

Chapter 14

"Socks," the town marshal said as the saloonkeeper rode up to them, "it looks kind of desperate when you need customers so bad you'll ride out after them." He spit at a rock the size of a horseshoe, hitting it dead center. "Wasted a ride though, we're on the way back."

"Ain't that, Frank," Socks said. "I know who done it, and I know where he is."

"That so?"

"Name is Sam Duncan. I recognized him from that poster you got up. He circled around and came back to town."

"Let's go, Marshal," the banker turned his horse.

"Hold on, Snodgrass. You know where we last saw his tracks. No way he's had time to get back to town yet. Duncan couldn't be the one that took your bank."

He looked at the saloonkeeper. "Socks, you sure about this being Duncan?"

"Sure as I'm sitting here."

The marshal turned his horse. "Bank robber or not, he's still wanted. Looks like the day may not be a total loss after all. Let's ride."

<>

Sam watched the meeting with interest from a little grove of trees next to the stream and the sound of the fat little man bringing up the rear reached him easily, but he couldn't make out the words. His manner suggested he didn't want them to go back to town.

"That's got to be the banker. He ain't interested in me; he's interested in his money."

As soon as they were out of sight, Sam headed down their back-trail. He had two reasons in mind. First, it was probably the way they would least expect, and second, it had occurred to him that the person who had held up the bank and his mysterious stranger just might be the same person. He didn't know what the odds were on that happening, but he didn't have anything else working for him at the present time.

<>

Logan had watched them turn back at the county line. He had counted on that, but couldn't be sure since some lawmen were more hardheaded than others. He figured to ease up his pace when he saw them do it. It was funny to see the little fat banker trying to change the lawman's mind. Logan didn't have to be within earshot to know that was what was happening.

Now what? He had money, had lost the pursuit, but was probably still too close to the incident back behind him. More distance was required. It was starting to get hot, maybe a little time up in the cool of the mountains of New Mexico would be a good idea.

As he rode, he pulled out the liniment he had stolen at the livery stable. He wet the corner of his bandanna again and bathed his sore neck. Every time he did this, his thoughts returned to the woman who had done it to him.

What kind of woman would take sure death over a little pleasure? Don't make no sense at all.

The liniment didn't burn as bad as it had been so he decided the cut wasn't as raw as it was. He reached back into his saddlebags to pull his shaving mirror. It didn't look too bad, but it was going to leave a really ugly scar. Man couldn't sew himself up without doing that. She had marked him for life. No matter, he smirked; he'd sure enough marked her for death.

<>

It wasn't much of a herd – a couple of milk cows, a bull, several calves fresh-weaned from their mamas and three more breeding stock for him. Pop was working on building his herd a little more at a time as he could afford it.

"Homer," Pop said, "you sure enough took your sweet time with these cows."

The cowhand looked pained. "Pop, it ain't like you can drive milk cows the way you drive range stock, and those calves ain't been off their mamas very long."

"Where'd you find those boys that helped you bring 'em in?"

The men that had been with him had drawn their pay and headed out as soon as they had the stock in the corral.

"Millers Run. They was at loose ends and glad for a few day's work. Say, who is this coming in?"

Pop turned around. He had a good idea who it might be. By the time the man got close enough for him to see the silver star on his chest with the circle around it, he knew he was right.

This had to be Stoker.

The ranger rode up to them, pulled up, and crossed his hands on his saddle-horn. "Howdy."

Pop stepped over and extended his hand. "Reckon you'd be Jake Stoker."

The ranger reached down to shake his hand. "I got a sign on my forehead or something?"

"You got one on your chest."

"It don't give a name."

Pop released his hand and stepped back a few steps. "It don't need to. Whatcha doing out this way?"

"Following a trail. Seems to come by here. Have you seen –"

Pop held up a hand. "Save your breath, Ranger, Sam was here. We fed him. We told him to stay and we'd hide him out. He wouldn't do it. He's a good boy."

"How could you possibly know that from just knowing him such a short time?"

"Ranger, there's some people you can know a lifetime and never have a clue what's going on in their heads. There's others you can spend five minutes with and you know what they're made of. Sam Duncan is like that."

"I see."

"Now I suppose you're gonna ask me where he went. You can do that if you want, but I'm either not going to answer or lie to you and send you the wrong direction."

"I don't need to ask, I know where he's going. I've already cut his trail going out."

"Then why are you here?"

"I'm not only hunting the man, I'm looking to understand him. I'd like to know why people keep being so very sure he's innocent."

"That mean you aren't going to take him back?"

"No, this badge says I'll take him back. You seen a man with a marled eye and a fresh neck scar?"

"So you've heard that? I take it you believe him then?"

"I didn't say that. But if I could find such a man, I'd sure admire to talk to him though."

Whittaker's wife walked up to them.

"Oh, Ranger, this here is my wife Hattie Whittaker. Hattie this here is Jake Stoker."

Stoker removed his hat and held it up against his chest. "William Jacob Stoker, Ma'am, Jake ain't a label my Ma hung on me."

"I'm sure it wasn't. Will you take supper with us, Mr. Stoker?"

Hattie's invitation was not so much a question as it was a statement of fact, no matter how it might have been phrased.

"I ain't had no home cooking in a coon's age, Mrs. Whittaker, if you're sure I wouldn't be imposing."

"Of course not. You can wash up over there."

They watched him walk toward the wash stand. She said, "What a strange man."

"Ain't many tougher men in the whole state, if there's any."

Chapter 15

Hattie set another bowl of red beans in front of Stoker. "You and Sam have something in common."

The big ranger looked up at her. "That so?"

"You both make the most of a meal when you get the chance."

Stoker smiled and cleaned his lips and his mustache with his napkin. "Ma'am, I'm sorry if I'm eating up too much of your groceries, it's just that this is the best grub I've had in a mighty long time and my appetite keeps wanting more of it even though my stomach keeps saying that I'm full."

"I'm not complaining, Jake, it does my heart good to see a man enjoying my food so much. I told Sam the same thing."

Stoker went back to work cleaning his plate. "Tell me about him, Miss Hattie."

"About Sam?"

"Yes. Both of you seem to have made an awful quick judgment on him. In my line of work, I find people ain't always what they seem."

"He's polite, generous, hard-working and when he told us about his mother, I could see the love in his eyes and face … and the pain. A woman knows these things, can sense them, he could have never hurt her."

"There's a powerful lot of people reading him that way. Some have known him all their lives, some like you and Pop only a short time. The sheriff believed he got a raw deal so much that he risked his badge to set him loose."

"Are you coming around to his side?"

"I don't get to have a side. I have duty to uphold this star no matter what." He smiled at her. "But sometimes knowing how a thing lays out can me help understand what needs to be done to insure justice is served."

"That's all we ask." She rose from her chair. "Did you save room for pie?"

"Not if you held a gun on me," he pushed back from the table. "But maybe after a little time to digest all this …"

<>

Sharon said, "It's driving me crazy."

She usually had sewing done for her, but now and then took a notion to try it herself, especially if the boredom factor got too high. She stood on a chair as Candace pinned up the skirt she had sewn up.

"Yes, I wish we knew something," Candace mumbled around the pins in her mouth. "Hold still."

Standing still was a difficult task for Sharon. "Do you think that ranger can find him?"

Candace stood back to look with a critical eye. It looked level to her. "They say he always brings back anybody he goes after, or he doesn't come back. I hear the men in the store talking about him as if he's superhuman or something."

"Oh, poo, he's just a man. Puts his pants on like any other man. I want to know if he'll really look for evidence or just drag him back."

"Hold still! You've made me pin my finger twice already. He said he'd keep an open mind, and he did promise to bring Sam back alive."

"Surely no man would ever say something they didn't really mean."

They giggled.

"I've been thinking of going to see," Sharon looked down to see if her friend looked shocked.

She did. "You wouldn't."

"I would if you'd go with me."

Candace shook her head slowly. "Our folks wouldn't let us. Take the dress off so I can finish hemming it."

Sharon got down and took the skirt off, careful of the protruding pins. "Daddy is on a trail drive. He won't be back for weeks."

Candace frowned. "My father hasn't gone anywhere. He wouldn't hear of it, and if I tried to go he'd come get me." She picked up the dress and started stitching the hem.

Sharon sat down at her dressing table and started brushing her lustrous hair. She closed her eyes, enjoying the sensation of slowly plying the brush. "I just don't think I can stand the waiting, not knowing. After all, the three of us have been friends most of our lives."

Candace looked at her friend without raising her head, a sideways glance. "Is that it, Sharon? Friends?"

"Well of course we're friends. What a silly thing to say."

"Not more? Just friends?"

Understanding dawned on her face. "Oh. I don't know. We've never–"

"You seem very upset for just a friend."

Sharon swung on her. "And you're not? Maybe I should be asking you the same question."

This would be tricky. The delicate balance of their relationship required that Candace know her place. She was not rich, didn't have Sharon's beauty, and played the role of the faithful minion standing in Sharon's shadow. Sharon flitted from boy to boy never seeming to form any attachments.

If Candace showed interest in a boy Sharon immediately overshadowed her. Maybe not intentionally, in fact she might not have even been aware she did it. She just had to be the brightest star in the galaxy.

Candace knew how she felt; she had feelings for Sam, but couldn't show them, couldn't let him know, and surely couldn't let Sharon know. That'd be like waving a flag in front of a bull. Almost inaudibly she answered, "We're just friends."

"Oh, I don't know what I'm going to do with you, girl. You never show interest in a boy. You're going to wind up an old maid if you don't come out of your shell. You should follow my example. Am I going to have to just play matchmaker and set you up with somebody?"

If it was the right somebody, Candace thought.

<>

Stoker rode slowly into Millers Run, practiced eyes scanning the sidewalks and windows for trouble. When you were a ranger who had faced as many men as he had, there was always trouble. He pulled up in front of the saloon and a man came out wearing the badge of a town marshal.

"Marshal," Stoker greeted him with a nod of the head.

Slade hooked his thumbs in his suspenders. "Reckon you'd be Jake Stoker. You're even bigger in person than I thought you'd be."

"My Ma set a good table."

"You here after Duncan? Or did you hear about the bank being robbed?"

The disinterest left Stoker's eyes. "Your bank was robbed? You figure Duncan did it?"

"The banker does. We heard he was in town, but the man we were chasing couldn't have gotten back that quick, so I figure he couldn't have done it."

Stoker folded his hands on the saddle horn. "Chasing? Didn't catch him?"

"I'm not like you, Ranger, I don't have jurisdiction out of this town. If I'd had him in sight, I'd have kept going, but all I had was a set of hoof prints to follow. I'm not even a full-time lawman, mostly I'm a blacksmith." Slade laughed.

"Not even sure what I'd have done with him if I caught him; we don't have a jail. Chained him to an anvil at the blacksmith's shop, I guess."

Stoker looked around. "I didn't see a blacksmith shop."

"It's part of the livery stable."

"Oh, anybody get a look at this bank robber?"

"The bank teller did. Not a good look since he had a bandanna over his face, but he said he had a marled eye."

That really did pique Stoker's interest. "A marled eye? You don't say."

"That mean something to you?"

"Maybe, maybe not. How about this Duncan? You said he came to town?"

"The saloon keeper come after me but he was gone by the time we got back. Trailed him down and into the creek, followed him downstream quite a ways. But never found anyplace where he got out."

Stoker looked in that direction. "You're sure he went downstream?"

"The posse was upstream chasing that bank robber. We'd have seen him sure if he'd come that way."

"There's nothing sure in life. How much did the bank lose?"

"This is a mighty small town, Ranger, mostly paper transactions on land and such. The banker figured it was a thousand or so."

"Appreciate the information." Stoker swung his horse.

He rode down to the bridge and dismounted. He knelt down to study the tracks. The Marshal walked over. "Checking up on what I told you?"

Stoker didn't look up. "I'm wondering why a man on the dodge rode through this soft sand to enter the stream when he could have ridden through the gravel over by the bridge. Man who knows what to look for could still find where he went through, but you can see the tracks he did make a long ways off."

"He was just in a hurry."

"Wasn't in too big a hurry to decide to ride in the stream. I figure he didn't want to do it just to keep his horse's feet cool. Man who does that is either trying to disguise where he comes out of the water downstream, or —"

Stoker walked into the stream, casting about. He walked over to look under the bridge.

"Some of these stones under the bridge have hoof strikes on them, fresh ones. You have many people hang out under here?"

"That's impossible. A horse couldn't go under that bridge, unless it was a pony."

"Tracks say different. Dunno how he got his mount to do it, but he sure enough did."

Stoker climbed back up the creek bank and remounted. "Looks like I'm following two trails and not just one. Convenient."

"Two to one? You want me to ride with you?"

"Ain't necessary."

The ranger turned upstream. He wasn't big on pleasantries or saying goodbye.

"You aren't coming in to eat?" Slade said, "or get a drink?"

"I'll take a hot trail over a cold drink any day."

Chapter 16

Sam followed Logan's trail up into the mountains, but he didn't know how far behind he might be. From what he had heard about the robbery he calculated it might be a day, maybe less.

He was closer than he thought.

Logan knew he had lost the posse, but a hunted man often takes time to scour his back trail and he did so now. He saw the lone rider come across the valley and enter the tree line.

"Well, well, what do we have here?" Logan said, "Lawman, maybe?"

Logan saw the rider dismount and work at reading tracks. There could be little doubt as to the quarry he was tracking. "We'll see who is following who," the outlaw said with a smirk.

He stayed well back of Sam, who was so intent on the trail that he didn't spend time studying his back trail as Logan had. He was unused to being a fugitive.

As dusk began to fall, Sam decided his best bet was to make night camp in a small clearing.

He built a tiny fire and busied himself making coffee and frying up some skillet bread. That suited Logan's purposes admirably, so he waited him out. When the task was completed, Sam sat down on a log to eat it.

That was the signal for Logan to step into the

clearing, gun in hand.

"I appreciate you fixing those vittles for me."

"For you?" Sam looked at the disfigured eye, the fresh scar on the man's neck. No doubt who this was.

"For me. You're not going to need it and there's no point in it going to waste."

The barrel of the gun didn't waver.

"Why am I not going to need it? I've done nothing to you."

"You're following me, that's enough, and don't bother to deny it, I seen ya reading my tracks."

Sam set the skillet and coffee cup on the ground. He didn't stand much of a chance looking down the barrel of a drawn gun. His mind raced, how could he at least take the evil man with him?

"You ain't even full growed. Why you tracking me?"

There was no point in lying. "You killed my Ma."

"The woman at that little ranch?"

Logan's hand went to his scar involuntarily. "That didn't have to go that way. We coulda had a fine time."

"You think she'd let you touch her?"

Logan's face took on a hard, sarcastic look, "Oh I touched her, all right, but it'd sure have been better for both of us if she hadn't gone all loco on me."

"I see she marked you. She told me she had."

"She paid for it."

Sam glared at him, unflinching. "You're going to pay for that, too."

"You figuring on making me pay?" The gunman laughed. "How fast you think you are? I got you covered like a blanket."

"If not me, those that are chasing me will do it."

"Why are they chasing you?"

"They tried me for the crime, but I escaped."

"Say, that means they aren't looking for me for it at all."

"If they ran across you they might start thinking about the description of the real killer that I gave them, even if I was no longer around to tell about it."

"That'd be real inconvenient, 'cause boy or not, you ain't gonna be around."

Sam knew he only had one chance, and that was surprise. He threw himself off the log backwards, clawing for his pistol.

Logan fanned two shots that hit the log.

When the pistol sounded a third time, it felt as if Sam had been hit in the head with a shovel. Fog flooded into his brain as he tried to bring his pistol up and take the man with him.

His muscles didn't obey him. I can't die and leave him alive, he thought, and then he succumbed to the darkness.

"Mighty tricky," Logan said as he stepped over to kick Sam in the ribs, then turn him over with the toe of his boot. The side of Sam's head was a mass of blood.

Satisfied, he picked up the skillet and coffee, still warm, and sat down to eat. "Never shot nobody before that made me a meal before I killed them."

He took a big bite and stared off into the darkness. "Wonder if this yahoo was telling the truth about somebody being on his trail."

He looked down at the body. "If he was, 'spect I don't want to be here with him when they show up. I want the trail to end right here."

Chapter 17

Dawn was breaking as Stoker rode into the clearing. The fire was out but tiny tendrils of smoke attested to the fact that it had not been out long. An unsaddled horse grazed peacefully a short distance away, but there was no sign of life.

Warily Stoker stepped down, pulling his colt. "Hello the camp," he said.

Normally he would have hailed the camp earlier if it hadn't looked so deserted. The tracks showed there had been someone else here, someone who had already ridden on. The smell of burned coffee lured him to the fire. There seemed to be evidence of a meal for one. Had a stranger come to the fire for a meal and been turned away?

Then he saw Sam lying behind the log.

"Well," he said aloud. "Looks like my trail ends here."

Stoker saddled Sam's horse in preparation for tying him on. He brought his men back, dead or alive. He shook his head; he hated to break his promise to such a pretty little girl, but at least it wasn't of his doing.

He took Sam's blanket to roll the body up in. As he rolled him over onto the blanket, Sam gave a small groan.

"What's this? Well, son, I think you might have a

little life left in you after all. This'll make a little lady mighty happy. Well, up until they send you back off to prison that is."

This called for a change of plans. Stoker built up the fire and heated some water. Gingerly, he cleaned the blood from Sam's head wound to get a closer look. Rangers had occasion to work with a lot of bullet wounds.

"Reckon if you were awake this would really hurt," he said as he dabbed at it with the hot water. Getting most of it clear he got down to take a closer look. "Son, I think you are one lucky son of a gun. I figured you to have a hole in your head and thought I'd find brains oozing out. It broke the skin, which is why it bled so much, but it looks like it bounced off that hard head you got."

He smiled. "If I was a betting man, I'd wager it saved your life. Whoever shot you intended to kill you, sure as the sun is gonna come up, it had to be that drifter you were trailing. If he hadn't thought he got the job done by all the blood and mess, he sure would have kept shooting until he was sure."

Stoker went over to his saddlebags to get a needle and thread to stitch up Sam's scalp. He also located Sam's saddlebags and rummaged through them. He found a clean shirt and took it to make a bandage.

He got down beside Sam to go to work. "I'm not a drinking man so I don't have any spirits for antiseptic. Guess you don't imbibe either, since I didn't find anything."

Just before he started, something caught his eye in the edge of the trees. "What's this?"

He walked over to find an empty whisky bottle. "Too bad," he said. He held it up to the light. "Then again, maybe there's a swallow or so left in the bottom. Looks like your luck is still holding, pilgrim, that's enough to dress your wound."

Stoker got his straight razor and cleaned the hair back from the wound. He sopped up what was left of the alcohol in part of the shirt tail he tore off and used it to sterilize the wound then he sewed the flap together with small tight stitches.

"Something else you're lucky about, son. My Ma didn't have any daughters, so I can sew a pretty nice stitch. I can also cook a passable meal and do a number of other things you might not expect. I really wouldn't want that to get around but I don't think you're gonna be telling anybody."

He finished by making a bandage from another part of the shirt with the alcohol soaked pad up against the wound. "Wasn't much of that redeye to do the job so this way we'll get the most out of what little we have."

He stood up and looked down. "Well, that's that. That ain't a bad job if I do have to say so myself."

Stoker cut some small saplings and fashioned a travois to carry the wounded man. If the boy could survive the trip back to Turkey Creek, he might have a chance. He surely wouldn't be able to make the trip all the way back, but one step at a time. Millers Run would do for now.

Stoker tied the long poles of the travois to the saddle-horn of

Sam's horse, loaded his prisoner gently onto it, then led the horse down the mountain taking it as easy as possible.

"I reckon you may still be dead and just not know it yet, pilgrim, but it ain't in me to take a chance away from you if you've still got one.

◇

Millers Run had no jail and only the part-time town marshal/blacksmith for law. How would he secure his prisoner?

Marshal Slade met him as he rode up. "Looks like you got your man."

"I always do."

"Looks like he put up a fight."

Stoker stepped down. "I think he did, but not with me. I found him this way."

Slade stepped to the other side of the horse to help untie the restraints on Sam. "Wonder who done it?"

"That, my friend, is exactly what's been nagging at me. He won't survive the trip back to Turkey Creek, though, so I'm gonna have to leave him in your custody."

"Whoa, Ranger, we got no jail, no doctor either."

"It don't matter, I got no choice."

Slade rubbed his chin in thought. "I guess we can bed him down in the livery, handcuff him to the anvil."

"You think that's necessary? He's out, he ain't going nowhere."

"I guess you're right. I'll just handcuff him if I'm going to be gone."

Using a blanket for a stretcher Stoker helped settle Sam into place. They tossed some fresh hay in a stall and carried him in to lie on a blanket. It took both of them to move the big anvil over to where the leg iron would stretch there from his leg. Stoker pulled his hat to wipe his forehead with the back of his hand, then walked back over to his horse.

Slade shook his head slowly. "You're not much for sitting around, are you?"

"I ain't got an ounce of patience, and that's a fact. I can't do nothing here so I'm gonna go run down your bank robber."

He swung up into the saddle. "Besides that there's another little matter I'd like to talk to him about."

He turned to ride out, then pulled up and turned in his saddle to look back. "You want to send word to Sheriff Fancher in Turkey Creek for me? Let him know we have Duncan in custody?"

"Sure thing, Ranger."

Slade watched the lawman ride out of town. He thought, that's the hardest man I ever saw. He motioned for Donovan to come across the dirt street. "Socks, you want to ride out and fetch Hattie Whittaker? She can do a little doctoring, and I reckon this jasper is sorely in need of some."

<>

Donovan rode into the little ranch at a brisk clip. Pop came out to meet him. "Hello, Socks, business so bad you're having to go off looking for it?"

"Why do people keep asking me that?"

"You're kind of a nocturnal creature. People just aren't used to seeing you in the daylight.

Socks's face flushed. "Oh har har, you're so funny."

"Oh, don't get all twisted up in a knot, I'm just funning you a little."

"I ain't got much of a sense of humor."

"So I see, what can I do for you?"

"The marshal sent me for Hattie."

"Whatever he thinks she done I can attest that she ain't been off the place for weeks."

"Aw, it's nothing like that; he just wants her to come do a little doctoring."

It wouldn't be the first time Hattie had been called on for that, particularly when somebody needed her to be a midwife.

"Who is it?"

"Some outlaw by the name of Sam Duncan. He got himself shot."

The humor left Pop's face. He turned and yelled, "Hattie … Hattie! You better get yourself out here!"

She appeared at the back door. "Hello, Socks, I didn't know we had company. Why don't you step down and…"

"Hattie, he ain't here on a social call, the marshal sent him for you. Sam has got himself shot and they want you to come tend to him."

The smile faded and her eyes got large. "What? When? "How …"

Pop took her by the arm and turned her back toward the house. "Plenty of time for that, right now you better get your stuff together while I hitch up the wagon."

"Yes, of course. And you'd better throw a mattress in as well."

◇

Pop and Hattie pulled their wagon up outside the livery stable and went in to get someone to care for the horse. There was no one there to do it, but Hattie saw Sam there, unconscious, chained to the anvil. She burst out the front door madder than a war chief on the prod.

Slade was having his lunch at the saloon when she blew in the front door like a hurricane. She's seen Duncan, Slade thought as he got out of his chair and removed his hat.

"Hello Miz Hattie, care for some lunch?"

"Don't you Miz Hattie me, you scoundrel. Why is that man chained up over there like a rabid animal?"

"Now calm down Miz Hattie. I only put the manacles on if I have to be away from the livery. I got to eat sometime."

"He's unconscious!" she screamed. "Where is he going to go? You go get those leg irons off him this very instant."

Slade looked down at his half-eaten steak and entertained a brief thought of telling her he'd do it as soon as he finished. He took one more look at her florid face.

He wasn't that brave.

As soon as they walked back into the livery, Hattie removed her wrap and went to work. Bright coals blazed in the forge, and it took Pop but a few minutes to produce some hot water so she could begin to tend to the wound.

She took the bandage off gently. "My," she said, "someone did a very good job of dressing this wound."

"It was the ranger," the marshal said.

She frowned. "The ranger? Is he the one that shot him?"

"Said he wasn't. He said he found him this way and tried to do what he could for him."

She nodded. "Then it was that man he was chasing. I was so afraid of this." She turned her attention back to Sam. "Look at these little precise stitches, I couldn't have done better myself."

111

She had some tincture of iodine to treat it, then put on fresh bandages.

Content that she had done all she could for now she turned her attention back to the marshal. Her eyes narrowed, and when she spoke, her voice could have had icicles hanging from the words. "I suppose there is some sort of reason you feel he should be in the stable like a mule instead of up in one of the rooms above the saloon?"

"We got no jail; putting him next to this anvil was the best I can do. I don't want to have to explain to that buzz-saw of a ranger how he got away from me."

"Would it not require him to be conscious to pull off such an escape?"

The marshal shifted his weight from foot to foot like a schoolboy being dressed down by the schoolmarm. "Yes, Ma'am. Like I said, I only put chains on him when I have to be gone."

"I'm referring to these unsanitary conditions, not his security as a prisoner."

She looked around the musty barn. He was lying in a stall with horses in the stalls on either side. Dust and chaff rained down from the hay-loft above. She stood and brushed off her skirt.

She made up her mind. "Very well, call over someone to help you and Pop place him in our wagon. I'll need to take him out to the ranch."

"I can't allow that." He had a look of distaste as he shook his head.

She spun on him. "You what?"

He melted under the fire of her gaze. "Now, Miz Hattie, I told you –"

"I've endured all of this foolishness I intend to put up with. You get someone over here and load him up before I really lose my temper."

"But, Ma'am, the ranger …"

She measured her words out like a fine recipe. "So it looks like you have the choice of making the ranger mad or making me mad. And you're just about there with me."

Oh, man, what a choice. The ranger might get mad, but then he was going to be moving on. Hattie on the other hand …

The choice wasn't hard when he got right down to it. "I sure don't want you mad at me, Miz Hattie. Let me corral a little help."

Chapter 18

Socks Donovan went directly from the Whittaker ranch to Turkey Creek to notify Sheriff Fancher of Sam's capture. As soon as that chore was done he headed immediately to the local saloon.

Within minutes, armed with juicy new gossip, Zeke Flagg began to make his rounds. It took him but minutes to make it to the general store where as fate would have it, both Sharon and Candace were visiting across the counter.

He eyed the shelf behind them. Business had been so good lately that he was getting pretty well stocked up. "How about a couple of those air-tights with peaches in them?"

Candace pushed them across to him, "Well?"

"Sam Duncan has been captured," he announced. "He's been shot and is near dead."

"What?" the girls said in unison.

Candace came around the counter, the color gone from her face. "But that ranger said–"

"Wasn't the ranger that shot him, it was somebody else."

Flagg loved to be the center of attention. He milked it, making the girls pry detail after detail out of him. When at last he was satisfied he had made the most of the opportunity, he went in search of a new audience. As soon as he left, the girls gave each other a

114

long look.

"That settles it," Sharon said. "We have to go."

Candace no longer seemed concerned about what her father would say. "Yes, it was different when we didn't know where he was or what he might be doing. He's hurt, he needs help."

"Daddy is still on the trail drive, I don't have to worry."

"My father would never let me go." Resolution set her face into a firm mask. "So I simply won't ask."

"Tell him we're going to finish sewing up that dress and you plan to spend the night with me." The girls often spent the night together, so she was sure this would raise no alarm.

"Yes, yes, that will work."

"I'll tell the cook I'm coming to spend the night with you for the same reason. It'll be a day or better before they figure it out."

"Sharon, you are deliciously devious."

"Aren't I though?" She gave her friend a mischievous smile.

Any reticence on their part forgotten, they completed their plans to leave. Candace's father never knew when the girls slipped out of town. They were on a mission.

<>

It worked. It was after noon the next day before Flagg came in making the rounds with the news of the two girls running off.

"She did what?" Ray Bates suddenly looked weak and leaned on his dry goods counter for support. Where had he gone wrong? "You're sure they left

115

town?"

"I'm sure. A couple of hands from the Circle J met them on the road. They knew who they were."

"What am I supposed to do?" Ray said. "I can't go off and leave this store; too many people depend on me."

"Perhaps I can help."

Ray turned to see the preacher standing in the doorway. "Brother Herbert, how can you help?"

"We're through here. We'll be heading that general direction anyway; I can track them down and see if I can prevail on them to come home."

The storekeeper's eyes pleaded with Herbert, "Would you, Preacher? I don't know what else to do. I'll send word to Colonel Delmar, of course, but other than that–"

"I give you my word. Perhaps for now we might get down on our knees and have a prayer for their safety?"

"Yes, of course. Of course."

<>

Washout was like most of the towns out here, a few buildings down each side of a dirt street with a saloon, express office, general store, and a small hotel that featured a full-length porch on the front; a porch where Logan sat in the shade nursing a drink. He watched the big red Wells Fargo coach come into town as if the devil himself were chasing it. How these drivers loved to make an entrance.

The bright yellow wheels pitched dirt clods as the driver threw his weight back into the reins and set the big brake rod with his foot. The loud "Whoa!" that he bellowed was as much to announce his arrival as it was to encourage the team to stop.

There were but two passengers, a gambler and his lady by Logan's guess. It wasn't the passengers, but the strongbox that drew his attention, however – specifically the fact that it took two men to get it down and carry it into the office of the stage line.

The stage always made its night stop there, but by the scheduled departure time the next morning, Logan was already outside of town, bandanna in place, ready to do his nefarious business with the coach.

He chose a spot a few miles out where the stage had to ford a small stream. The driver would slow up for the crossing at least, and if he was lucky, would stop and let the horses have a small drink of the cool water.

He was lucky.

He got a small bonus as the shotgun guard stepped down to get a cool drink as well. Logan stepped out of the brush. "Both of you lift those hands, and don't do anything stupid."

The guard looked at the double-barrel gun peeking over the edge of the driver's box. Indecision played across his face.

"Man ought to do what he thinks best," Logan said.

The guard made up his mind. He wouldn't do anything stupid.

The driver pulled his pistol with two fingers and dropped it over the side.

"Now that double-shooter."

The shotgun followed, then the express box.

"Anybody inside?"

"Just had two passengers coming in and they

stayed in town."

Logan shot the lock and loaded his saddlebags with the contents. He had the driver dismount and then stampeded the horses.

"I can't believe you did that," the driver whined.

"They'll quit running here in a bit and you can catch up to them. If not, people from town will come out when they get back there. Either way, it's going to be a while before anybody takes out after me."

Chapter 19

The girls rode into the little ranch. Pop got up from where he had been sitting on the porch as they made their way over to him. He removed his floppy old hat as introductions were made.

Sharon said, "I wonder if we might water our horses?"

Pop smiled. "You girls come in and refresh yourselves. I'll go water and cool your horses."

They were glad to do so. He helped them down, and Hattie met them at the door to take them into the kitchen. By the time Pop came stomping in the door, slapping dust off his clothes with his hat, they were sitting around the table with a hot cup of tea in front of them.

"I've told you a thousand times to do that outside, Horace."

He smiled. "And I've answered you a thousand times that I started the process outside."

"And I've told you an equal number of times that you should finish it outside as well."

It was obviously a well-rehearsed and long practiced exchange, more playful than serious.

He plopped down in a chair and Hattie set a hot cup of coffee in front of him. "I don't mean to be nosy, but you girls are very young to be traveling by yourselves."

Sharon scooted forward in her chair, excitement showing in her eyes. "We're on a mission. A friend of ours was unjustly accused of a crime. Now we hear he has been injured and we're rushing to take care of him."

Pop and Hattie exchanged looks. "You don't say," he said. "And what would this friend's name be?"

"Sam Duncan. We have no idea how we will go about finding him, but we're quite determined to try."

Candace said, "I think if the Lord intends for us to find him, He will provide a way."

Sharon leaned forward to take Pop into her confidence, "Candace is a bit of a religious fanatic."

"I am not," a pout developed on her lower lip. "Having Christian beliefs doesn't make me a fanatic."

"Be that as it may," Pop said, humor toying with the corners of his mouth. "I wouldn't go making fun of her beliefs until after I went over there and looked behind that door.

It was the girls' turn to exchange incredulous looks. "You mean he's here?" they said in unison.

"In the flesh."

The two jumped up and ran to the bedroom. Clean and airy with lace curtains on the windows, it was a far cry from the dark and dusty stable with horses switching flies with their tails in the stalls on either side. Yet neither arrangement made any difference to Sam; he was still unconscious.

Candace's hand went to her mouth and her eyes became moist. "Is he hurt bad?"

Hattie came up behind her and put an arm around her shoulders. "It's hard to tell with a head wound. I'm no doctor, but I've tended many a cowboy who has been kicked in the head or had a gun barrel bent over his skull."

"But a bullet–"

"Just like getting hit really hard if it doesn't go inside the skull, and this one didn't."

"I reckon whoever shot him thought it had," Pop added, "or they would have finished the job. They surely intended him to be dead."

Candace nodded slowly. "It was that evil man he was chasing, it had to be."

"Sure could be. A man ought to be really careful what he chases lessen he catch up with it."

<>

Stoker knew what he was going to hear before he even got to Washout. His practiced eye had seen the jumble of tracks on the road where the stage had been stood up. He saw where the horses had been stampeded and two men left afoot, men that had been picked up several miles from town.

As he rode up to the man wearing a star that stood waiting on the boardwalk, he thought he'd save some time. "Looks to me like you had a holdup, Sheriff."

The man looked incredulous. "Now how could you know that? And I ain't the sheriff, he's over at the county seat. I'm just the local deputy."

The deputy didn't have to be told the identity of the man he was talking to. The silver star and circle said he was a Texas Ranger, and everyone had heard the description of the legendary Jake Stoker.

The explanation was brief but thorough. Stoker ended it with a question. "You seen a man in town with a marled eye? Fresh scar here on his neck?"

He made a motion with his thumb to indicate the

position of the scar.

"I seen him over at the hotel. Ugly cuss. Looked like he was patched together out of two or three different men with all them stitches all over him. He disappeared about the time the stage was held up, and I wondered about that. We took a posse out but had to give up when we hit the county line."

"He seems to count on that right heavy."

"You thinking he's the one that took the stage?"

"I am." Stoker swung down. "And a bank over at Millers Run, probably more. I don't figure him to be new at this."

The man was long enough gone that the need to give chase was not immediate.

And he was hungry.

Chapter 20

Candace and Mrs. Whittaker took turns sitting by the bed. Sharon said she couldn't function without her beauty sleep. On the third day, Candace was deep into a catnap when a voice jolted her awake.

"Candace? Is that you?"

She came awake, jumped to her feet and covered the two steps to the bed in a seamless motion.

"Sam, how do you feel?"

"Like I've been kicked in the head by the world's largest and most ornery mule. How did I get here? Isn't this Pop Whitaker's place?"

"It is Pop's place, and it wasn't a mule, you've been shot."

Candace pulled his bandage loose gently. The abrasion seemed to be healing nicely. She told him so, but told him the worst of it was the doctor that had come in from Turkey Creek had said he had a concussion.

"What's a concussion?"

"I asked him that, and he said it was an injury to the brain."

Sam seemed to having difficulty processing the information. "That sounds really serious."

Candace shook her head. "He said it was temporary, but that it'd cause headaches that could be debilitating. He said it could even cause amnesia, or at least trouble remembering things or making decisions."

"I guess that's true, I'm sure enough having trouble getting things to fall back into place. Wait a minute, you said I was shot. Who shot me?"

He winced as she secured the bandage back into place.

"According to that Texas Ranger, it was the man you were chasing."

"How would he know?"

Candace sat on the edge of the bed. "He read the tracks, he looked at the evidence, maybe he read some tea leaves. Who knows how he's able to figure out so much about those he is pursuing? Good thing he found you though, he was the one that first stopped your bleeding and first patched you up."

"Reckon I'm in his debt. So, it was the man with the marled eye? I got that close, huh?" Then it dawned on him. "Hold on, did I hear right? Ranger? Stoker was here? How come I ain't under arrest?"

"Actually you are," a deep bass voice said.

Sam and Candace looked toward the door to see the big form of Slade seeming to fill the door frame completely. The lawman walked in the door and pulled some manacles from his belt. He snapped one end on Sam's wrist and the other on the brass bed frame.

He rose up and smiled a humorless smile. "I thought you might be coming around. I don't reckon you'll be going anywhere chained to that bed, not until Sheriff Fancher gets here to pick you up anyway. I sent word to him."

Candace gave him her most sweet, disarming smile, "Marshal, that isn't necessary."

"Don't bat them big eyes at me, gal. I think it is

124

very necessary. I didn't get here none too soon. I 'spect he's got too much head on him to fork a horse now, but another day or so and he'd be out of here."

He put his hand back to his hip pocket. "Speaking of which, the Doc over in Turkey Creek sent you out this bottle of laudanum. It'll get you through the next couple of days. He said it oughta start letting up by then."

Slade set the bottle on the table by the bed. Sam eyed it as if it were a live snake. "That stuff will knock you out, won't it?"

"It'll make you not care whether you're awake or asleep. For most people that means right to sleep."

"Then I don't want any right now. I can put up with it until I find out what's going on."

"Your call."

Slade turned to go into the other room. They could hear him calling out as he went down the hall. "Now, Mrs. Whittaker, how about that piece of pie you offered me as I came in?"

His voice awakened Sharon from her nap. She immediately breezed into the room. "Well, look who's awake."

Sam looked bewildered. "Sharon? You here too? What's going on?"

Sharon moved over to fluff his pillow and straighten the covers. "When we heard you had been shot, we came running, of course.

"But why?"

"Don't be silly."

Candace came in the door to see Sharon fussing over Sam. They failed to note the small scowl that passed over her face. While Sam had been out, Sharon had not worked with him at all, leaving the chore of sitting up with him and tending to his needs to her.

But let him show signs of life and look who shows up as if she had been there all along, Candace thought.

"Mrs. Whittaker is keeping the sheriff busy with deep dish apple pie."

She moved around to the other side of the bed. "We have a few minutes to talk."

Sharon looked at her, "Talk about what?"

"Talk about getting me out of here," Sam leveled his gaze at Candace. "You have an idea?"

"Don't be talking foolish." Sharon said. "The sheriff isn't going to take his eyes off you. What you need to do is go back and clear yourself."

His voice took on a tone one would use to explain things to a child. "I tried that once, remember? It got me sentenced to Territorial Prison. I have to go find the man with the marled eye, or prison is where I'll be going."

He returned his attention to Candace. "I asked if you had an idea."

"I might have."

Candace scooped up the Laudanum bottle and left the room.

<>

There was nothing glamorous about man-hunting. There were those who had joined the Rangers expecting it to be all excitement and action. They hadn't counted on days on end of tedium trying to pick up a trail – the unending process of scouring the countryside looking for a hoof print in soft earth, a broken twig, a scraped rock, to talk to someone who had seen something and could provide a direction.

Hunting a man took patience, dogged never-give-up patience, and that was what made Stoker the best. There were few dictionaries out in this wild country, but had anybody found one and looked under the word "patience," it might well have had the picture of Sergeant William Jacob Stoker beside it.

Down on one knee, he worried over the shadow of a hoof print.

"That's him," he said aloud.

Men who spent a lot of time alone often spoke aloud,
sometimes pretending it was to their horse, but generally it was the need to generate sound in the silent country.

"That Cayuse of his throws his left front foot a little."

He stood, and swung back in the saddle. "Reckon I'm still on his trail."

He rode off in the direction the track pointed, reaching back into his saddlebag to pull out a piece of jerky and a cold biscuit. That eating place back in Washout had made good biscuits and he had bought all they had ready. He'd eat in the saddle, and if his quarry stopped to cook a meal he'd make up more time.

<>

Down the trail, that was exactly what happened as Logan built a small fire to heat up some beans and fry a little fatback. He had seen no one on his back trail, but could not rid himself of a nagging feeling that the ranger was there.

A man on the run didn't run in a straight line. If he

did, he was soon scooped up like a fish in a net. No, he doubled back, changed directions, and didn't take the obvious path. Logan had done all of that, and his tactics should be enough to take out the average pursuer.

Logan took the skillet and walked to the edge of the rise to slowly scan the countryside.

Can't hurt to be careful, though. There are those who just don't fall into the average category.

Chapter 21

Candace swept into the kitchen with a rustle of petticoats. She scooped the coffee cup off the table with a bubbly "More coffee, Marshal?"

The lawman glanced toward the room where his prisoner lay handcuffed to the bed. "Well I oughta . . ."

At the cabinet, Candace pulled the Laudanum bottle from her apron and poured a healthy dollop into the cup, diluting it with steaming hot coffee. Mrs. Whittaker saw what she was doing and hopped up to cut the marshal another big slice of pie.

"A big man like you can't fly on one wing. I know you can eat a second piece."

"Oh, I shouldn't." The sheriff finished his sentence by patting his stomach, but his eyes were already devouring it.

"Of course you can."

She set it in front of him and he went to work on it in a workmanlike manner.

Candace replaced the coffee cup at his elbow. He paused in between bites to take a sip. He made a sour face. "Thing about eating something sweet, sure does make coffee taste bitter by comparison."

Mrs. Whittaker looked hurt. "Maybe I best make a new pot."

He held up a hand in protest. "Nothing wrong with the coffee, Ma'am, just that it can't stand up to comparison with nectar like this pie."

He continued to alternate between eating and washing it down. The women exchanged smug looks. Candace wondered how long it would take it to do its job.

The peace officer drained the last of the cup, stood and wiped his mouth with the back of his hand. "Mighty fine groceries, Mrs. Whittaker, but I've got a job to do."

He ambled back into the room and dropped heavily into the chair by the bed. Sam closed his eyes when he heard him coming and feigned sleep. Sharon headed into the kitchen to find out what was going on.

"I'm glad you left the room," Candace said. "It's best it be very quiet in there."

Sharon didn't have to say it; it was written all over her face, but she said it anyway. "I don't understand."

"I've given the marshal a taste of Sam's Laudanum; I'm hoping it will knock him out quickly."

"If he goes to sleep as quickly as Sam did, it won't take long."

Candace smiled. "I doubt Sam is really asleep."

Hattie said, "The marshal is going to be mad."

"He'll get over it."

They gave him ten minutes then went to check. Marshal Slade sat in the chair with his head drooped at an impossible angle.

"He's going to wake up with a really sore neck," Candace said.

She gently nudged the sleeping officer, but got no response.

Sam was not asleep. "The key is in his vest pocket."

Candace removed the key and unlocked the

manacles. Sam rubbed his wrist trying to restore circulation. He hopped up and quickly pulled pants over his long johns. He scurried toward the barn pausing but a moment in the kitchen to give Mrs. Whittaker a hug for her part in the deception.

He threw his tack on his horse, mounted, and walked the animal out of the yard so as to not make noise. The girls walked beside him to the gate.

"I reckon I could be leaving with a brass band and it wouldn't make no difference," he said, "but it don't hurt to be safe."

He tipped his hat to them. "I don't know how to pay what I owe you."

Candace smiled and gave him a pat on his leg. "There's no need."

He swung the gelding and put spurs to him. In a moment, he was gone.

◇

The marshal slept for two hours. He awoke to find his charge gone. He jumped up and ran through the house, finding all three women apparently asleep. He roused them.

"Where's Sam? What have you done?"

Mrs. Whittaker said, "Whatever are you talking about, Marshal? We've lost a lot of sleep sitting up with him. Since you were here, we took advantage of it to catch up a little on sleep ourselves."

He eyed them suspiciously, but they looked so innocent, so naïve.

Surely they couldn't …

He shook it off. It didn't matter. He had to get after him. "Well, he can't get far in his condition. I'll catch him up before nightfall. I have to or that ranger will have my hide on a plate."

He made his way to the barn and saddled up. His head hurt something fierce, as if he had a hangover.

I ain't been drinking. What's going on? Gonna be hard to make any time with it pounding this way.

"What's the matter, Marshal?" Candace said with a concerned look on her face.

"My head is pounding something fierce, and my neck feels like it's been tied in a knot."

"What you need is a cup of coffee."

<>

"I thought that was your horse in the corral."

Sharon jumped to her feet. "Daddy, what are you doing here?"

The Colonel had come in so quietly it had caught them all by surprise. "I might ask you the same question."

"It's a long story, and I asked you first." Candace watched her friend take the defiant pose she affected when she was about to get her way no matter what.

"Don't take no book-learning genius to see the drive is over and I'm on my way home, and I've got time for a long story. But it better be a good one what with two young girls off by yourselves this way."

Mrs. Whittaker led them into the kitchen and put a piece of pie in front of him at the table. Both girls began talking at once, yet he seemed to be following it all, shifting his eyes from one to another, chewing and savoring each bite. The pie and the story wrapped up at the same time.

"Another piece of pie, Colonel Delmar?"

"No thank you, Mrs. Whittaker, though it was a treat from the gates of heaven itself. After all, from what I've been listening to, a second piece of pie around here comes at a certain risk."

Mrs. Whittaker smiled her appreciation at the little joke and busied herself cleaning up the dishes.

The Colonel turned his attention to the girls. "I guess I can't fault you for standing up for a friend that way. When cowboys ride for the brand, they do whatever is necessary to protect the ranch and each other. Reckon I couldn't expect less from my daughter."

The fatherly pride was clear as he looked at Sharon, then it changed to a look that was all business, as did his voice.

"But the notion of you two riding after him at your age is pure foolishness. You're coming with me, so get your things together."

The girls exploded into animated discussion. He ignored them.

"I reckon I may take that second piece of pie after all, Mrs. Whittaker. It appears I'll have to wait out this little squall."

He got up. "I think I will pour my own coffee though."

The arguments beat upon him like surf on the rocks, with about the same success. He finished, pushed back to wipe his mouth with a napkin, and said, "Every bit as good as the first, Ma'am." He turned his attention to the girls. "Git your stuff. Do it now."

Unexpectedly, Sharon suddenly became meek and obedient. This was a side of her that Candace had not seen before. Apparently Sharon was headstrong and a force to be reckoned with only until her father put his foot down. It caught Candace up short.

"It's too late to leave now," Mrs. Whittaker objected. "You will hardly get down the trail before you have to overnight. You might as well spend the night in a bed."

The Colonel nodded. "I have to say the idea of a real bed after weeks on the trail is not something I find objectionable."

She smiled. "I have a bed that has recently been vacated. I'll put fresh linen on it."

The Colonel put his horse in the corral and tended to him. The remainder of the evening he regaled them with the adventures from the drive just completed, but it ended when he announced that he was rather tired. They all turned in to be able to get an early start in the morning.

They never knew when Candace left.

Chapter 22

The big wagons that Herbert and Peggy drove suited their life on their road spreading the gospel. They lived in the first one, and the second carried a small pump organ and the materials they used to set up a church in each town. The wagons rattled their way through the gate and up to the house.

"Here now, what's all this?" Pop said, coming down the steps.

Herbert pulled up and doffed his hat. "Ladies. Good morning to you too, gentlemen. Allow me to introduce myself. I'm Herbert Green, and this is my wife Peggy."

"Traveling preacher, eh?"

"You have a good eye, Sir. Yes, we take the Lord's word wherever we feel He directs us to take it."

Herbert looked at the girl on the porch, recognizing her from the tintype he had been shown back in Turkey Creek. "You would be Sharon."

Suspicion clouded the face of both Sharon and the Colonel. The Colonel descended the steps, still holding his cup of coffee.

"And how would you be knowing that?"

"Storekeeper back in Turkey Creek asked me to be on the lookout for two girls and showed me a tintype of them. I presume Miss Candace is somewhere about?"

He looked around the tidy little ranch, wondering why she hadn't made her appearance.

The suspicion left the rancher's face. "I fear she is farther than we would like her to be. We got up this morning to find her gone."

Herbert didn't appear surprised. "Then my mission is but half satisfied."

"My name is Robert Delmar, Sharon is my daughter, so I relieve you of any responsibility toward her."

He turned to look at the suddenly petulant girl. "She will be traveling home with me today."

The Colonel turned back to Herbert. "I had intended that both girls make that trip, but I underestimated her quiet little friend."

"Glad to meet you, Mr. Delmar. I'm glad your daughter is safely in hand."

Hattie swept forward. "Colonel, can't all this wait until we get these dear people down from these wagons and seated in front of some breakfast?"

Pop introduced his wife and then himself. "You might as well step down," he added. "Ma ain't much on taking no for an answer, and for her, food and hospitality are one and the same."

Hattie took Peggy into the house as Pop and Herbert unhitched the teams and put them into the corral. They dusted themselves off with their hats as they came in. Herbert said, "The storekeeper is going to be really put out when his daughter doesn't come back with you."

The Colonel nodded somberly. "That he will."

"You can tell him I will still honor my word and try to catch up to her. I fear we won't have any better luck at making her return than you did, but we can at least keep an eye on her."

"I will pass that word to him, I know he will be grateful. I know I am that you were willing to take the time to look for my daughter even if it did not turn out to be necessary."

"Happy to do it."

Pop took the chair next to him. "Preacher, you going to be holding a meeting around here? We're mighty hungry for some good preaching."

Herbert glanced at the Colonel and did not see the same enthusiasm. Perhaps there was work to be done here. "I would like to, but time would seem to be of the essence."

He looked at the eager faces of the two Whittakers. "The small number gathered here reminds me of a town we visited this past winter. There was a howling blizzard, and we were holed up most comfortably to wait it out. Yet when the time for the services came, I noted someone had come into the tent and seated themselves."

Pop's interest was aroused. "You don't say?"

"I do say. I figured if he had made the cold trip to come in that I could at least make the trip in from the wagon. I went out and ascended to the podium. I didn't shortchange him, but gave the full sermon that I had planned."

"Mighty good of you." Pop nodded.

"I thought so too, but following the sermon I asked the man what he thought."

He said, "You know, Preacher, if I go out to feed my stock and only one old cow shows up …"

"Yes?"

"I don't dump the whole load."

The kitchen echoed with laughter. Pop said, "So

you figure you shouldn't dump the whole load on such a small herd as you have here?"

"My point exactly."

Hattie set a big slab of pie in front of him. "Maybe you could just give us a little taste of it, if you can do that and eat at the same time."

"You make a very tasty argument."

◇

"Ma'am," the man said, removing his hat as he rode up to Candace. "Forgive me if'n I seem forward, but you appear to be a mite lost."

"I am most certainly not lost."

She straightened her backbone and lifted her chin. "I know exactly where I am and where I am going." Her face softened a little. "But I admit I might could use some help in the best route that it might take to get me there."

He smiled. "Maybe I could help with that. My name is Homer Coble. I work for Mr. Whittaker over at the Flying W."

Candace seemed to lower her guard. "How interesting. I just came from there. I believe I did hear your name mentioned, and that you were off doing some work."

"Work is a kind name for what I've been doing. Now about this route you were talking about?"

"Yes. I am trying to catch up to a friend of mine, and he is rushing to catch up to someone else."

"That sounds pretty complicated," Homer said. "So where is it this first man is headed?"

"I believe he is headed for the border."

Homer looked as if he had bit into something

138

distasteful.

"Ma'am, the country between here and the border is no place for a lady riding alone."

"I do not intend that I should be alone for long."

"How far ahead would this jasper be that you are trying to catch up with?"

"He has less than a day's lead on me, and he is recovering from a wound, so I expect he is not riding as hard as he otherwise might."

"Well, I ain't met nobody," Homer rubbed the back of his neck as he thought, "but I can't in good conscience let you ride off down that way alone."

Her chin went back up. "There is nothing you can do to stop me."

"Oh no, Ma'am, I didn't figure I had a shot at that, but I reckon Pop would forgive me if'n I delayed my return long enough to ride with you until you catch up to your friend. In fact, if I tell him I met up with you and didn't ride with you, he'd be powerful mad."

"I have no intention of allowing a strange man to ride with me. I don't know anything about you."

"That's a real sensible attitude." He pulled his pistol and handed it to her butt first. "How about if I give you my gun and you can just shoot me stone dead if I make a false move?"

She took the gun. "I suppose your intentions are honorable enough."

He crossed his heart with a finger. "Pure as the driven snow, Ma'am."

He turned his horse. "I did see some tracks going southwest a while back. That's the right direction, so I figure we might go back and see where they take us."

Chapter 23

Sam knew he had done the right thing, knew that fate had left him no choice. At the same time he feared – no, he absolutely knew – he had bitten off more than he could chew.

He was sweating profusely and had no doubt he was running a fever. What bothered him most was the fact that he could no longer trust his eyes. He was having hallucinations, seeing all manner of things that were not there.

There was nothing new about mirages in this desert country, and when he had seen a couple of waterholes that turned out to not be there at all, he didn't think anything of it. But when he started seeing large jackrabbits walking upright, nonexistent houses and waiters carrying trays of food and beverages, he knew he was in trouble.

He leaned over in the saddle to ask the large rabbit where he might replenish his water supply, but once he started leaning he couldn't stop. He hit the ground hard and lapsed into darkness. His horse gave him a sideways glance, then being used to the strange actions of humans, walked a short distance away and began to graze.

◇

Stoker looked down at the tracks, then sat back into the saddle, crossing his hands on the saddle-horn. He looked off into the distance as if he could see the faraway rider. He had tracked so many men that he could get into their heads, understand their thoughts. He tried to do that now.

"You're just jerking me around," he said as if the man could hear. "You're going to lay down a trail in that direction until you think anybody following you has bought it, then you figure to swing around for the border again."

He swung his horse. "Well, I ain't going for it. If you do that, you're going to find me waiting for you just outside of Slow Dog Pass. If you don't show up, I'll know you have to be heading back to one of two towns, and I'll be wearing out horseshoes getting there next."

The ranger trotted his horse heading for the line of low mountains where he hoped to intercept his prey. They were further than they looked, and the sun started to get low in the sky before he rode into the foothills. He knew the exact place where he needed to make his play and went directly there, hoping he had beaten his quarry.

Stoker stopped on the ridgeline and dismounted. There were no fresh tracks on the trail below so perhaps he had made it. He pulled a pair of Army binoculars from his saddlebags and squatted on his heels to painstakingly study the horizon, sitting gingerly because of the rowled spurs threatening his backside.

He studied the landscape slowly, methodically, then came to a stop. There it was, a small dust cloud over to the east. He permitted himself a tight-lipped smile. A dollar will get you five that's this man with the marled eye, he thought. He replaced the binoculars into his saddlebags and pulled out a small coffeepot. He figured he had an hour yet. He put the pot back. What am I doing? If I can see that dust plume, he could see a fire, no matter how small I made it.

<>

"There's a horse grazing over there," Homer pointed to the animal.

"Oh. That's Sam's horse."

They rode over and quickly found him lying by the trail. Candace ran to him and sat down to pull his head into her lap. Sam awoke and looked up. Another hallucination, but this one was pretty. He closed his eyes again.

Homer bent to look him over. "He looks in a bad way."

"Yes," she wiped sweat from Sam's forehead with a dainty handkerchief. "He's running a fever."

Homer straightened up and pointed. "There's a waterhole down there in the valley. Reckon we ought to tote him over there."

"How do we do that?"

"It ain't far. Can you carry one end of him?"

"I think so."

Homer took his blanket and a couple of poles and made a makeshift stretcher. "I'd make a travois for the horse if it was further, but this'll be much quicker if we can carry him all right."

They could, and did. They got him into the shade of some short mesquite bushes beside the shallow waterhole. Candace started bathing his face, neck and chest with the cool water as Homer tended to the stock. He came back with some little envelopes in his hand, about the size of cigarette papers.

"This here is some headache powders. Had a couple of them in my saddlebags. These and that cool water is about all we can do for him now. I surely do hate to leave you alone, but I reckon the smartest thing for me to do is ride the hide off this horse going for a wagon to tote him back to the ranch."

She nodded. She had come to the same conclusion.

Homer built a small fire and left a stack of wood by it. He built it some distance away so the heat would not compound Sam's problem.

"Gotta keep him cool now, but come nightfall, we can't let him take a chill. Reckon this wood will last until I get back."

"I don't know how to thank you."

"Thanking people doesn't enter into things out here, little lady, folks just tend to one another." He swung back into his saddle. "I'll be back as quick as I can."

With Homer gone, it became quiet, but it wasn't a peaceful quiet; it was almost unbearably silent. She could even hear the grinding of teeth as the horses chomped on grass a short distance away. She felt so unbelievably alone, even with Sam's head lying in her lap. Her chest was tight, constricted, what if someone, something . . .

She forced the thought from her mind. She could handle it, she could protect Sam.

She felt a new strength wash over her like a liquid. A new feeling for her; she had always been so dependent on others. She rather liked it.

"Candace?"

She looked down into the big brown eyes in her lap. The glassy look was gone. She felt his forehead; it felt cooler. His fever was down. He was not out of the woods by a long shot, but the powders and the cooling water were helping.

"Hi, Sam."

"I thought you were another hallucination. I can't believe you're here."

He tried to raise his head. "Sharon?"

"Lie still," she said harshly. "There's nobody here but me."

"What?"

He tried to get up, but she held him down with ease. "Out here alone? Have you lost your mind?"

"A cowboy helped me get you over here. He's gone for a wagon to take you back."

"I can't …

"You can't do anything right now. I know you don't want to go back, but that's out of our hands right now."

He accepted the inevitability of her statement. "I can't believe you're here. I guess it wouldn't have surprised me to see Sharon, but . . ."

Candace's eyes blazed. "You men are all alike; all you can see is the glitter. Sharon is a show pony, bred for the ring. She catches your eye, dazzles you and it lasts until she gets interested in someone else. Do you have any idea how many cowboys have their cap set for her? And she encourages each and every one of them."

"But she came to the jail and . . ."

"She's a friend, and a good one. Don't you know how to tell the difference between friendship and something deeper? She came with me, was flirting

144

with that sheriff while you were laid up, and as soon as her father laid down the law, she trotted right back home with hardly a whimper."

"I saw her flirt with the sheriff. I thought she was just trying to get on his good side to help me."

"You men always see what you want to see."

"I wish you'd quit lumping me with 'men' as if it were some sort of evil club."

"Not at all, men have wonderful qualities, but they have some obvious shortcomings."

"I've noticed over the years that neither men nor women can be counted on to be logical when it comes to their love life."

She suppressed a small smile. She had never heard him use the word love before even as a passing reference unless it was in connection with his mother. "So are you trying to tell me something about your love life?"

"I don't have a love life, though I have had thoughts of perhaps working in that direction." He appeared very puzzled. "And Sharon sashayed back at the drop of a hat, while meek, mild little Candace continued on determined as a bloodhound? That's a notion that takes some getting used to."

"Oh, I give up. You can't see what has always been right under your nose – who it is that has always been there for you."

Chapter 24

Logan rode unsuspectingly through the pass. He caught up short when he heard a cold voice say. "Rein that horse in, and keep those hands where I can see them."

The outlaw lifted his hands as instructed. He didn't need to be told who this was. "You have to be Jake Stoker."

"I suppose I have to be, got no choice in that. You pull that iron with your left hand and let it drop to the trail."

Logan complied. He knew the ranger's reputation and knew better than to try anything, not now anyway.

"Now get down, on this side."

The horse danced a little, unused to anybody dismounting on the right. Logan kept his hands high, continuing to hold the reins.

"Now tie him off, and don't try to get around behind him or I'll figure you're up to something and will just go ahead and shoot you."

Moving with molasses slowness, Logan complied, then turned to wait for the next instruction. Stoker crossed behind him and lifted the Winchester from the scabbard.

"You look like a hideout man to me, where is it? You don't want me hunting it myself."

Logan gingerly removed the pocket revolver from

his boot.

"Now the knife," Stoker gestured with the big Walker Colt in his hand.

The knife clattered on the ground.

"Reckon that pulls your teeth. Gather up some wood, I hanker for a little coffee before we head back."

The fire and coffee made, they sat beside the fire. Stoker said, "I figure you to take a short drop on a long rope for all you've done. But what I'm not sure of is the lady back in Turkey Creek, tell me about her."

Logan eyed the ranger. One thing he didn't need was for some lawman to be all upset at him over the way he'd handled her. "I don't know what you're talking about."

"That lady's son said you killed her. Described you to the last hair on your head."

Logan shrugged, "I heard he done it and is trying to lay it off on me."

Stoker covered him while he built the fire and put the coffee on. They took each other's measure over the tin cups as they drank.

"You got nothing to lose by telling me the truth," Stoker said finally. "I got you on more than enough as it is."

"I'm telling you the truth. Why would I lie?"

"Most likely just because you can."

Stoker got up and put the fire out with the last of the coffee.

He put the pot back into his saddlebag, pulling out a pair of manacles at the same time.

"Tighten your cinch back up and mount, and don't do anything stupid. Be easier to shoot you and tie you over that saddle than to mess with you, so don't tempt me."

Stoker tossed the manacles to him. "Put those on."

Logan caught them, then both men jerked at the whirring sound at Stoker's feet. The ranger jumped back and shot the snake's head off with a single blast. His horse went one way and he went the other, fought for balance on the edge of the rim, teetered, then went over the side.

Logan tossed the handcuffs to the ground and ran to pick up the ranger's rifle where it lay by the fire. He could see him lying below. He maneuvered, but couldn't get a clear shot.

"Ah, he's done for. I ain't gonna waste a couple of hours riding around to get down there."

He shoved the ranger's rifle into his scabbard. He'd like to have his pistol back, but it was in the ranger's saddlebags and there was no telling how far that horse would run after the encounter with the snake.

<>

"Oh, I'm so glad you ran into her," Hattie said. "I was so worried."

"Well, she's all right," Homer said, "but I can't say as much for her boyfriend."

"I was afraid of that." Hattie shook her head somberly. "Pop, why don't you hitch up the team while I get a little food into Homer."

"No need in you going," Herbert said. "I have to go anyway, I gave my word. I'll pick him up, then we'll see where we need to take him from there."

"It's a shame Sharon and her father have already gone. We could have sent word to Candace's father."

HOUNDED

They hitched up Herbert and Peggy's wagon and prepared to continue after her. Herbert gathered the little group into a circle, holding hands as he invoked the Lord's protection for Candace and Sam and over them on their journey.

At the end, Pop smiled sheepishly and said, "I ain't much used to hand holding."

Hattie smiled at Herbert. "Now that's a fact."

<>

Sam's fever had indeed broken. Candace had dipped into the meager supplies she had eased out of Hattie's kitchen and had boiled up a hearty broth.

"This tastes mighty good, I didn't realize how hungry I was. But to tell you the truth, I think I could handle something a bit more substantial."

"In a bit. Your body can convert this to energy much faster than something that needs to be digested. Get as much down as you can and I'll fix you something more substantial after while."

Her logic rang true to him and he sipped and drank all of the liquid he could hold.

"You really let me have it while ago," he said over the rim of the cup.

She flushed scarlet. "I don't know what came over me. It's as if it had all built up and just boiled over."

"I'm glad you got it said. I have been taking you for granted. But it's more than that; somehow you seem different, more self-assured."

"I've had to do things I didn't think I could do, take care of myself." She looked down, unable to maintain eye contact. "I like how it made me feel. In the span of only a few days, I think I may have changed."

"It shows on you; and I like the way it looks."

"They'll be coming for us soon," she changed the subject, uncomfortable with the unaccustomed flattery. Flattery was Sharon's province, not hers.

"Yes, and I can't go back; it'll be all over for me if I do."

She poured the last of the broth into his cup. "You aren't up to going on after that man, but there's another choice."

"Another choice?"

"Let's leave now and go to California. It's not far to the border, and that ranger wouldn't follow us there. We could take the Mexican route to California."

"We?"

She made and held eye contact. "Yes, we. You still need help and I'm willing to see you get there. You haven't expressed any feelings for me, and I'm not asking you to, but if you'll go, I'll go with you."

Sam smiled. "Now who is not being logical about her love life?"

"I didn't say anything about love." The eye contact broke.

"Nor have I. All this is still pretty new to me, and I'm not sure we're old enough yet to—"

He sighed deeply, losing his train of thought. "I ain't sure I've wrapped my mind around it all the way yet, but I know I couldn't take care of you the way things are. I am seeing you in a new light though, is that enough for now?"

"You talk like I'm trying to drag you down the aisle or something. I never thought any such thing. I'm just willing to help you get away."

"Even so, I can't take you up on your offer though

it sure means a lot that you made it. But I know about Stoker and he has a reputation for never giving up on a chase. That Mexico border won't mean squat to him, and running away will just make me look guilty. I have to face up to this and clear myself, but I have to do it out here, if I let them take me back I'm through."

Chapter 25

Stoker's head seemed on the verge of exploding. He managed to fight to a sitting position and put his hand to his forehead. What happened?

He fought to clear his mind. Slowly it came back to him, the snake, the fall, he looked up. How in the world did I survive that?

He saw the small scrub cedar growing out of the side of the rim. His bandana still hung on it. It had broken his fall. He struggled to his feet.

"I reckon the Lord still has some use for me down here after all, 'cause he sure could have had me there if he'd wanted me."

He began limping to the gap, hurting in places he didn't even know he had. When he came out of the ravine into the open he put two fingers into his mouth and let go with a piercing whistle.

Stoker went to his knees, hands on either temple. That was excruciating. "Man," he said aloud, "I hope that silly horse heard that, because I don't think I can do it again."

Or maybe Logan took his horse. If he was afoot out here he really had a problem. Then he heard a familiar whinny.

"Horse," he said, "I don't know when you've ever looked so good."

He pulled into the saddle with some effort. Once

aboard, it took several minutes for him to be able to breathe normally, for the pain to subside to a manageable level.

He turned the animal and headed after the outlaw, at a gentle walk that wouldn't jar his aching head too badly.

As he rode, his mind was busy. The boy's story was starting to look good to him. Sure, Logan had denied killing the boy's mother, but that wasn't surprising. Still, what he thought and what he could prove were different things. He'd do his duty; he'd take the boy back. He'd even speak up for Sam, but proof was proof, and the law was the law, and Stoker would always back the law no matter what he thought.

"Best thing I can do is catch this galoot and take him back," he said aloud. "Pick up Sam on the return trip and hope a jury will see it his way. The evidence points to Sam, though it's hard to tell if a jury will see it different than they saw it the first time. Hard to say."

<>

Logan had reversed course again. He worried that Stoker may have communicated where he was headed and told people Logan was hotfooting it to the border. There might be others in the area after him. He decided the best bet was to again backtrack and take a different trail to the Rio Grande.

He rode steadily for several hours, then took a slight detour to a waterhole he knew about to water his horse. There was someone there. He dismounted and walked his horse in so he could approach quietly.

Logan said, "I thought I already killed you."

Candace gave a startled gasp as she and Sam spun

to see the outlaw standing over them.

"No matter. I'll take care of it now and this time I'll be sure."

He leered at Candace over by the campfire. "And this is quite an added bonus, a chance to have another woman with nobody around. Things are looking up."

Sam gave a primal roar and made a play for Logan, but the outlaw clubbed him to the ground with an almost casual blow from his rifle stock.

Candace said, "What do you mean 'another woman'?"

He laughed. "Why this boy's momma, of course. Fine looking woman she was."

His hand went to the scar on his neck. "Unreasonable though. I hope you're a little more sensible."

He turned back to Sam, levered the Winchester and pointed it to his head. "You made a good try, boy. I'd have done the same thing, would have given it one last chance, but …"

Bright lights went off in Logan's brain. Candace had slammed him with a rock before he could pull the trigger. He went down hard.

By the time he struggled back to consciousness, he was tied up like a calf at branding. Candace was across from him again working on Sam with cold compresses.

"I don't know when I'm going to quit underestimating women," Logan said with a smile that had no humor in it.

Her anger blazed at him when she looked up. "He was just starting to recover. That blow you gave him may have been too much."

"Oh play some violin music, I think I'm gonna cry."

The disgust she felt dripped from her words. "How can one man be so unspeakably evil?"

"Practice, lady. Years and years of practice."

"Hummmph."

"So now what, lady? You've got a real problem. You can't nurse that boy back to life and keep an eye on me, too. You sure enough can't take me back by yourself and do that as well."

She looked at him, weighing the truth of his words. "There's another choice."

He looked amused. "And what would that be?"

"I can just shoot you."

The amusement erupted into laughter. "Like you have it in you to do that." But his voice lacked conviction. He had just finished saying he had a habit of underestimating women.

Candace got up and faced him. She cocked the rifle. She was clearly thinking about doing it.

He decided he'd better do something and do it fast. "Of course, doing that would never clear your boyfriend."

"You admitted you did it; I have your confession."

"You tell them that. Nobody will believe you. Everybody will think you're lying to cover up for him."

Indecision played across her features. He followed up on it. "You know I'm telling the truth. I bet you said you believed him at his trial, didn't you? Didn't do much good, did it?"

"You're just trying to confuse me."

"You know better, I can see it in your eyes. You know I'm telling the truth, they'll never believe you."

She aimed the rifle at the middle of his chest. "The old Candace could never shoot anybody, but all I've gone through lately has changed me. I'm not the girl I used to be. I can and will do it." She pulled the Winchester tight to her shoulder. "And I can make them believe me."

Chapter 26

Sweat poured down Logan's forehead and into his eyes. When was he going to learn to leave women alone? They were his undoing every time. He looked in her eyes and had no doubt. She was ready to pull the trigger.

His voice gave away his desperation. "How about if I can offer you a way out? A way that won't force you to kill me?"

The rifle didn't shake or waver. "I'd rather not have to kill you, but I'm not turning you loose."

"How about if you leave me tied, take my weapons where I can't hurt you and can't follow you? In this country, that is probably sure death anyway, but you wouldn't be the one that was doing it."

She didn't trust him. "I would think you would prefer a quick end to that."

"No, that way I at least have a chance. I might live long enough for you to send the law back for me. That might even offer your boyfriend a chance to be cleared if I did live."

And more important give me a chance to get out of these ropes and get out of here, he thought.

Candace lowered the rifle. She liked the sound of that. It could work.

"All right, but I'm taking your horse, too."

"What?"

"That's the only way I'll consider it. If you get loose you'll be afoot."

She was afraid to remain there with him but didn't want to kill him. The answer was clear, go back and meet the wagon somewhere back down the trail.

"That's a death sentence for sure." This time he wasn't saying it just to con her.

It was the best she was going to do. He resigned himself to it, at least he would be alive, that in itself offered him some outside chance. He watched her gather materials and build a travois.

"How'd you know how to do that?"

"I've heard of them. I've never seen one, but I understand the concept. Two long poles up to the saddle-horn on the horse, then make a little platform back here. I may not be doing it exactly right, but I'll bet it works."

"In all honesty, I couldn't do no better myself."

She made a face at him. "What would you know about honesty?"

"I know it when I see it. Never had much use for it myself, you're sure enough right about that."

She stopped to admire what she had done. She was pretty sure it would do exactly what she needed it to do. Almost casually, without even turning to look at him, she said, "Why did you kill his mother?"

"She cut me."

"You deserved it, but surely that didn't merit death."

"Lady, I've killed people for looking at me wrong."

She couldn't fathom the kind of evil that would allow a man to make that kind of statement, much less make it in a manner so devoid of emotion. Human life

158

meant absolutely nothing to this man. But now she had another problem. She couldn't lift Sam up onto the travois.

"Turn me loose, and I'll put him on there for you. I'll let you tie me back up after I've done it."

She ignored him. She stood there, hands on hips, assessing the situation. Then she got the coil of rope from Sam's horse, tied it under his armpits, got on her own horse and slowly pulled him up onto the platform. She knew it must have hurt or scratched him up, but it was all she could think of.

"You're giving me a whole new outlook on the subject of womenfolk," Logan said. "I'd have never thought of that. You are one smart, savvy female."

"I have to admit that I've been doing things the last few days I didn't know I could do. I'm stronger than I ever knew I was."

"You don't have to prove it to me. Not long ago, I took down the toughest Texas Ranger anybody ever heard of and you have me trussed up like I was going to market."

"You killed that ranger?"

"Nothing to it, he wasn't so tough."

"That's terrible."

"It also means he's not on your boy's trail any more."

"Yes, there is that all right, but it was him I was counting on to come back and get you after we leave."

"Life don't always work out the way we plan."

Before Candace was even over the hill, Logan rolled into the waterhole. Wet ropes should loosen up enough that he could get out of them, but what then? He lay in the water, slowly working to stretch them. The travois couldn't move very fast and would be a cinch to track, even at a run.

Who am I kidding? I can't run that far and that long. What would probably happen would end up with him running into the cowboy coming to meet them, and him unarmed.

No, he was going to have to find a way to go the other way and head for the border.

But first he had to get out of these ropes.

<>

Stoker followed Logan's tracks into the waterhole and found Logan already gone. He wet his bandana and tied it around his aching head, then settled down to read the tracks. There had been two people at the waterhole, one a woman. He saw one seemed to be injured and the other had fashioned a travois. Not knowing Sam had escaped the ranch, he had no reason to suspect the truth, but he could see it was the man who was injured.

Good thing this lady was gone by the time Logan got here or she'd have really been in trouble. No way a little gal like that could handle him. Now I got to catch up to them before he does, or she'll still be in trouble.

He swung back into the saddle, this time not waiting for the pain to subside, but reining the horse around, he headed out at a trot. The travois could be tracked at a pace as fast as his horse could run, but he picked a pace the mustang could keep up all day.

It didn't take that long. Candace was trying to go slowly and as gently as possible, riding around things she might have gone over if she had just been riding by herself.

She saw him coming, and by the time he got there, she was standing out with a cocked rifle in her hands.

160

He held his own hands high. "Easy, little lady, I'm downright peaceable."

She scowled. "I didn't recognize you at first.

"Yes, Ma'am, but you don't seem to be putting that gun down now that you do recognize me."

"No, you're still set on taking Sam back."

He gave her what he hoped was a conciliatory smile. "I don't mean to be picky, Ma'am, but aren't you heading back yourself?"

"I suppose so." The rifle barrel dipped. "Logan said he killed you."

"You've seen Logan?"

"Back at the waterhole. I hit him with a rock and tied him up. Did you kill him?"

He lowered his hands but made no offer to step down. "Nobody was at the waterhole when I came through."

"That means he has escaped, but he has no weapons and is afoot so he should be easy to apprehend."

"From what I've heard so far, I expect his tail-feathers have been singed a mite. Men, particularly men like Logan, don't take well to being bested by a slip of a girl."

"I have come to understand of late that I am not a slip of a girl."

"No, Ma'am, I can surely see that."

She was suddenly all business. "I need him caught, Ranger Stoker. He admitted to me that he killed Sam's mother, but he also said in an unguarded moment of truthfulness that people would probably not believe me if I told them that."

"There may be truth to that all right."

"Then it is essential that he be returned with us

and forced to tell the truth."

The change in Candace became more and more pronounced as her anger kindled. The mousy little shopkeeper's daughter was gone, and it was beginning to look as if she was gone for good.

Stoker turned sideways on his horse, looping his leg around the saddle-horn. He pushed his hat back on his head with his forefinger. "That leaves me with a little problem. Now that I have Duncan in custody, I can't turn him loose to go chasing somebody else."

"You do not have Sam in custody; I do. And surely you have noticed the speed at which I must travel."

"I have, but I'm also aware that Logan is traveling at an even slower speed. Custody or not, I can't go off and leave you in this sort of fix."

She was clearly annoyed. "Why is it every man in the world is so sure that I can't exist without his personal protection?"

"Never thought any such thing, Ma'am, but neither do I think it should be any harder or more dangerous than absolutely necessary."

Chapter 27

That fool ranger has nine lives.

Logan had watched as Stoker came into the waterhole and tended to his wound, then puzzled out the tracks. He doesn't know I'm afoot, so he isn't looking for me here. If that little maverick female hadn't taken my guns, I could put a stop to this right now.

He had been forced to watch the ranger ride off unmolested. Under the circumstances, there was nothing else he could do.

He struck off down the empty streambed, since it was easier walking.

Water came down these streams on occasion and would be impounded in ponds along the way after it passed like a highballing freight train. Logan approached such a pond now. A caterwauling noise intended to be singing came from the body of water, and out in the center, a man wearing his hat and a pair of what once must have been red long johns was occupied taking his spring bath.

There was no necessity of removing the long johns as they needed to be washed as well.

A short distance away, a little sod house was built back into the creek bank. It was a convenient way to build a quick house except for the minor inconvenience caused when one of the five-minute floods came downstream, but that didn't happen often. Logan took the man's boots without being seen, then slipped into the house and helped himself to the man's food and weapons. He loaded his plunder on the man's horse and rode out, oblivious to the indignant yells coming from the pond.

Salamander Jack Fargo was not a man to take a slight lightly. He turned the air blue with new and inventive ways to string cuss words together every time his bare foot hit the ground coming out of the water. In country where a man was considered old at the ripe age of 40, it would be difficult if not impossible to put an age on the old trapper. He seemed as ancient as the mountains.

Hair and beard of a salt-and-pepper black turning gray both fell on his chest and back, encircling him, making him look for all the world like a face peering out of a bush. He had the potbelly mandatory for his age where his chest had slid down into his drawers, but he wasn't fat. Living such a sparse life filled with hard work from first light to can't see didn't lend itself to putting on padding.

Salamander Jack continued his invective upstream to his cabin. A sailor would have been taking notes. It stepped up a notch as soon as he saw all that was gone; most of his food, blankets, the man had left him little of value. He pulled on an old pair of moccasins and some old clothes, right over the wet long johns. He'd dry quickly enough, maybe from the inside out as hot as he was.

He surveyed what was missing, threw a meager kit of possibles together and went out to pursue the offender. To do this required the services of an old, half blind donkey. He shook his head sadly as he approached the animal with a blanket to pad the donkey's bony back.

"I'm sorry, Little Bit, I know I done promised you could retire and live out the rest of your days in peace, but that varmint has left me no choice. You know I got to git after him."

The apology went on and on as the pair rode after Logan.

There was no point in chasing the man; the donkey wasn't up to it. He didn't have to track him; he knew where he had to be going. Besides, he was not well equipped for the trail and the first order of business was to provision himself.

And get some boots, he thought. What kind of man would leave you with no boots?

Jack led the donkey up over the ridge. A short way down the valley, he found where the man had discarded his boots. He also found where the man had relieved himself in the bushes and was stunned to see what he had used for paper.

"Donkey, I don't shake out to be much of a believer, but it'd take a pretty low life varmint to use a Holy Book this way. Even heathens that have no use for preaching generally respect The Book.

"I don't know what we're chasing here, but it don't shape up to be anything like I ever come across before."

<>

Herbert and Peggy didn't know how much further ahead Candace might be, but they were losing their light. They decided to night camp at a little grove of trees. They pulled the wagons in close to set up the campsite. They each had their chores, and turning to the mundane tasks helped set their minds more at ease.

They soon had the wagon in position, a nice fire going, and a couple of their tent meeting benches set up by the fire to sit on. An iron tripod had been set up over the fire and a big cast iron pot hung down over it, flames licking around the base. A coffeepot stood at the edge of the fire on a little nest of coals Herbert had pulled aside. Wonderful smells wafted from the big pot.

"Hello the camp!" a voice called from the darkness.

Herbert moved over to pick up his rifle. "Who's there?"

"It's Jake Stoker."

Herbert put the gun down as soon as Stoker's face was visible in the light. "Come in, Jacob, and welcome."

He peered past him. "You have someone with you?"

Candace rode into the light leading a horse with a travois attached to it. Peggy ran to her. "Child, we've been so worried about you."

Stoker stepped down. "You may have been worried, but you can take my word that little lady is no child. She's done a heap of living since you last saw her. This outlaw I was chasing done got the best of me, but she took him down like he was nothing."

Peggy looked shocked. "Oh my."

Candace pushed her hair back out of her eyes. "I had a confrontation with him back at the waterhole. Can you believe it ended with him tied up like a Christmas package?"

Herbert laughed. "Astonishing."

Peggy led Candace over to the fire. "Would you men quit cackling like sitting hens and carry that boy over here by the fire?"

"Don't take a woman long to get things in hand, does it?" Stoker said as he turned to do as she had instructed.

They took Sam from the travois and bedded him down near the fire. Peggy came to place a hand on his forehead. "He feels a little hot to me."

Candace said, "That horrible man hit him with a gun. He was running the highest fever I ever saw, but it broke. It still comes and goes a little."

"How long has he been out?"

"All day. He needs something in him if I could get him awake long enough for him to take it."

"The stock in the stew would do admirably when he's ready."

Herbert looked down at her. "We've been praying powerful hard that the Lord would protect you, Sister, and it appears he has."

Stoker looked up over the rim of the coffee he had just poured. "I don't want to make light of your faith, Preacher, but I'd have to say the little lady had to pretty much take things into her own hands."

The corners of Herbert' mouth turned up almost imperceptibly. "That so? Does it strike you as sensible that a slight little thing like her should be able to best a man you yourself said got the upper hand on you?"

"Now I'll give you that one, Preacher. It don't make a lick of sense."

"God works through people, Jacob. Many times when we find ourselves doing things we simply aren't capable of doing, it's because we have help."

"You may be right." They looked down; the voice

had come from Sam.

"Well now," the ranger said, "look who has come back to the living again. You're a hard man to kill."

The ladies rushed over to tend to him. They propped Sam up a little and began to spoon stew stock into him.

The men fell on the stew like ravenous wolves. In between huge bites, Stoker said, "Preacher, I've got to take out after that snake that done this. I'm figuring the boy will travel much better in your wagon than on that bumpy travois. But there's one thing, I got to have your word that you won't let him get away from you."

"I'm no jailer."

"Be that as it may, I got to have it or I'll take him with me, travois and all. That couldn't do him much good."

"You leave me no choice."

"None at all."

"Very well, I give you my word that I will keep him here with me. Though in his present condition I hardly think that is a problem."

"I didn't think it was a problem when I left him back at that ranch either."

"Point taken."

Chapter 28

Salamander Jack knew the short way.

He didn't know if the man was headed for Runnel's Crossing or not, but it made sense that if he wasn't, he would eventually. Still, even though he felt like he was sure to be ahead of the man, he entered town like an animal sensing a trap.

He circled the main street to come up on the livery stable from the back side. His horse was not there. He turned the donkey into a stall, rubbed him down and gave him some feed, then slowly and painstakingly poked around town until he was sure the man was not in evidence.

Then and only then did he go to find the sheriff to lodge a complaint. Salamander Jack was a man that took things in order, one step at a time.

In a thrown-together little border town like Runnel's Crossing, being a lawman was not a full-time job. Sheriff Monahan also owned the livery stable as well as running a flock of goats and used them to make cheese. Cowboys liked cheese, but mutton was something a cowboy seldom, if ever, had a hankering to eat.

Jack found the sheriff pouring goat milk into a cheese mold. "Put your badge on, Sheriff, I want to swear out a complaint."

Monahan liked doing the sheriff's job; it offered a

welcome diversion from an otherwise boring existence, as long as there was no actual danger involved, that is.

At those times, the whiny little lawman tended to have urgent business at the county seat. Something about the old trapper's tone alerted him to the fact that such a trip might be in order.

"What's the problem?" He didn't look up from the task of putting the coarse cloth over the top of the mold, securing it in place.

"Thieving varmint stole my horse and dang near everything else I own."

Monahan saw a possible out. "Out at your place?"

Jack spit a stream of dark brown tobacco juice. "Of course at my place."

The whining tone of Monahan's voice rose until it sounded almost feminine. "Dagnabit, Jack, you know I don't have any jurisdiction outside the city limits."

"Of course I know that, you old fool, but lessen I miss my guess, he's going to come riding right into the middle of your jurisdiction."

Monahan was afraid of that. "When?"

"I got no idea, but he'll come through here, I'll bet my new saddle on it. Course, if'n he don't come through here, I won't have my new saddle back to pay off the bet."

"Well, I do have a trip to the county seat planned–
"

"Aw, I ain't counting on you and that useless piece of tin you wear, I just wanted it on the record so when I shoot him and get my horse back, nobody will be looking crossways at me."

"As long as it's a fair fight."

"It'll be fair. I plan on hiding behind something

where he can't see me and blowing him out of his socks."

"Sounds fair to me."

◇

Sam fell asleep again, the men turned in for the night, and the women lingered over a meal of stew and cornbread. Peggy analyzed Candace's face in the firelight. She looked somehow older.

"When I met you back in Turkey Creek, I never dreamed you capable of going on an adventure like this. Your friend Sharon maybe, but not you."

"No, you would have been right."

"So what happened?"

"Sam happened."

"Really?"

Candace made a gesture of resignation. "He needed help and nobody was giving it to him."

"As simple as that?"

Candace blushed. "I suppose not. I care for him. I have for a long time."

"But he doesn't see it, right?"

"How did you know?"

"Men are silly creatures. They're drawn to beauty and never seem to realize that beauty doesn't last, character is what lasts. I could see her overshadowing you, like a moon to her bright star. Don't worry, they usually wake up and see what they should have seen all along."

"Maybe he already has. We've talked of it a little, very little, but some. I think it was when she went meekly trotting home with her father that he realized things weren't quite what he thought they were."

"Only talked a little?" The significance of the

phrasing was not lost on Peggy. "So he hasn't gotten anything said?"

Candace sighed deeply. "Not at all."

"You know why, of course."

She nodded. "It's all new to him; he doesn't know how he feels yet."

"Yes, that's part of it." Peggy reached out to put a hand on her arm. "The bigger part of it is the fact that he doesn't have a future to offer you. As sure as I'm sitting here, he doesn't want to allow himself to think about what he might have with you as long as he's in the situation that he's in. Absolutely wouldn't want to lead you on and then have you stuck pining away for him while he's locked up the rest of his life, or worse."

Candace set her plate aside. "Suddenly, I'm not hungry. You really think that's it?"

"I'm sure of it. We've got to help him get his future back. Then maybe he can think about what might be between you. But

Candace…"

"Yes?"

"Don't be in a hurry, all right? Most of your life is still ahead of you. You may feel like you know what your feelings are, and you may be right, but take the time to be sure."

<>

Stoker left at first light. He didn't know anything about Salamander Jack, but nonetheless his thinking had reached much the same conclusions as Salamander Jack's had come around to.

He'll circle. He'll play games, but eventually he's got to head for the border. In this part of the country that'll be Runnel's Crossing.

He spurred the horse. If I don't play those games and just go straight there, I should be able to get there first.

Ahead of Stoker, Logan had left clear tracks for an entire day headed back toward the Texas hill country. He ate breakfast with some hands working cattle, let them see him riding east, then when out of sight, entered a small stream and turned west, riding in the water. He had laid a nice trail, and it was time to head for the border.

Eastern folks coming out West had trouble getting it in their heads that people in this wide-open country knew one another. They would live in their tightly packed environments and maybe not even get to know more than a handful of the people around them.

In this wide-open country where a man could see campfire smoke, dust plumes, or at night a campfire light from as far as 30-40 miles away, people knew when somebody was around. Traveling the country meant utilizing known waterholes, which meant trails that were used.

All travel meant going through the few towns that existed, and the travelers immediately availed themselves of the one point where they could find out any dangers that might exist, waterholes that might have dried up, or just exchange news for the entertainment value of it. In other words, drinking man or not, they headed to the saloon where they met people and where they talked about others they had met and where. For a place that looked like hundreds of miles of nothing, people knew a lot about who was doing what and where.

Back East it would be far too much coincidence

for isolated trails to cross, and folks might pass within a block of one another and not know it. In this country, for the paths of Salamander Jack, Stoker, Logan, and the Green party to come together; it would not be coincidence, it was even likely if not inevitable.

◇

Things very often look better in the morning. Sam spent a fitful night with Candace and Peggy taking turns sitting up with him, but the light of dawn found him awake, fever down, and more alert. Predictably, he immediately started having thoughts of resuming his search.

"You want to do what?" Candace couldn't believe her ears.

"Don't act so surprised, you know what I have to do."

"I understood it when you seemed to be mending. I know you feel it is your only chance, but getting hit on the head again in almost the same place took away all your progress. I'm surprised your brains aren't so scrambled that you can't even think. Come to think of it, maybe they are, or you wouldn't be talking this way."

"Awful early in the morning to be shouting so, isn't it?" Herbert walked up to them with the coffee pot and a couple of empty cups in his hand.

Candace looked contrite. "I'm sorry, did we wake you?"

"No, it's time to be up. Y'all want some coffee?"

They nodded, and he handed over the cups and poured them full. Sam sat more upright and leaned against the side of the wagon he was in to accept his.

"Couldn't help but overhear," Herbert said. "Sam, you know I gave my word to Jacob. I'm not going to let you ride out of here, even were you up to it, which you aren't. This little lady is right. The ranger was willing to take my word on that, and I honor my word. Now I'm going to have to ask you for your word that you won't try to escape."

The two men held each other's gaze for a long time before Sam answered. "I know you got to keep your word. I also know what I got to do. I hope that doesn't set us against each other."

"Don't be in such an all-fired hurry to kill yourself. If you try to ride with that concussion you are bound to have, that's what you'll be doing, you know? Maybe there's some common ground for now and we can worry about it later.

"We're going to have to make it to a town and re-provision, ply my trade a little since I'm not just out here traveling around for my health you know. I suppose this town that Jacob is headed to would be as good as any, and you stand a better chance of getting there in this wagon than you do trying to ride."

"All right, that'll do for now."

"Let me say again that I need your word you won't try anything different."

"You'll take my word?"

"Of course."

"I give you my word I won't try to ride out of here without talking to you before I do it."

"That's good enough for me."

Chapter 29

"Sam, did you mean what you said?" Candace sat next to him in the wagon, her eyes boring into his.

"I always mean what I say, I don't know no other way."

"So you meant what you said when you told me you were seeing me in a different light?"

Sam grinned. "I wondered how long it'd be before you got back to that."

"To what?"

"To us."

Her heart rate quickened. "Is there an 'us'?"

"No."

A shadow passed over her face, disappointment, shock, maybe some of all of it.

Then he finished his sentence. "But there could be."

Her head came up, hope in her moist eyes. "Could be?"

"I got no right to even think of such as that right now. When it crowds to the front of my head, I push it back, shut the door on it. I don't have a future myself, much less one to offer to somebody else."

"Peggy said that's how you were feeling, that you wouldn't express yourself to me until you thought you were free of your troubles."

"No kidding? She's a smart lady."

"She also said we shouldn't be in a hurry, that we're young with our lives ahead of us and we should take our time and be sure."

"That sounds like sound thinking to me."

Candace got very quiet, then finally said, "But what about Sharon?"

"Sharon? She hasn't crossed my mind since I heard she headed back with her pa. I guess it took that to get me to see she was just a pretty bauble, a nice decoration for somebody's Christmas tree. I was kinda dazzled by her, I suppose."

"All men are. I used to like to be with her because, I don't know, I suppose some of the attention rubbed off on me too."

He took her hand and kissed it, held it up against his chest. "Her beauty is all on the surface, yours is bone deep."

Her breath became shallow, she felt giddy. "Beauty?" she said softly.

"Are you saying nobody has ever told you you're pretty?"

"My father."

Sam threw his head back and laughed, a short burst followed by his freezing in place as wave after wave of pain washed over him. Time froze until it passed and he could slowly open his eyes.

"Whew, I never knew that laughing could be a painful experience."

She put her other hand on top of his hand as it still held hers captive. "I'm sorry, I didn't mean to cause that."

She looked puzzled. "Although I don't know why that was so funny."

He touched her cheek. "You are beautiful, you

always have been. You've just been so shy and retiring, that people don't see it. They didn't see you, particularly with Sharon stealing the spotlight so."

Candace hadn't moved on, she was still stuck on one sentence. "Nobody has ever told me I'm beautiful."

"I expect you're going to hear it a lot. You weren't kidding when you said you had changed, you know. There's a new confidence in you, a self-assurance that really looks good on you."

<>

Logan rode into Runnel's Crossing slowly, as was his custom. His eyes took in the entire town at once, alert to any danger. He saw none. He didn't even see Salamander Jack hanging out down at the end of the street like an over-the-hill guard dog. Jack immediately ducked out of sight. He needn't have bothered. Logan had paid him no heed back at the cabin and surely wouldn't have recognized him had Jack walked right up to him.

He watched as Logan rode directly into the livery stable to get his horse off the street. The outlaw stripped his saddle from the horse and settled him into a stall.

Before Jack could formulate a plan of action he saw Stoker ride slowly into town, reining up at the hitching post in front of the saloon.

"This won't do," Jack muttered. "That varmint will spot that ranger's horse and be off for the border before the ranger has a chance to grab him. Even if I trade for a horse, that'll put me chasing him down into Mexico."

The old trapper rushed off behind the buildings. "This won't do at all."

Jack slipped around to the back of the livery with a skill born of years of hunting and tracking. He eased up the ladder to the hayloft, no plan in mind. Below him, Logan finished seeing to his horse, threw his saddlebags over his shoulder, pulled his rifle to carry casually in his left hand, and headed for the door.

Jack was in no position to do anything, and Logan stepped through the door and into the bright sunlight. As Jack had feared, the outlaw saw the horse and stopped in his tracks.

Logan's mind churned, processing the information, but before he could turn back into the stable, Stoker stepped out of the saloon and spotted the outlaw immediately. It was too late to run for it, the stage was set.

Logan didn't want to shoot it out with the ranger; he'd heard far too much about the big man's prowess with a gun.

If he tried to get back inside the stable and shoot it out from cover, chances are he'd never make the door. Any move, and the ranger would surely draw and fire. He didn't seem to have many options and all of them looked really bad.

Stoker stepped down off the porch, walking directly toward the outlaw. It was not his way to wait on trouble.

His words echoed the outlaw's thoughts. "You got no good way to go, Logan. You got one chance to live, and that's to toss down that gun and give it up."

He continued to come nearer and nearer. If he had a chance at the longer range, the lawman could not miss as close as he was now.

Indecision has killed me, Logan thought, but he couldn't let himself be taken back, that would be sure death as well.

Maybe, just maybe –

The outlaw's hand swept to the Navy six in the cross-draw holster.

His brain didn't have time to register on the shadow falling over him.

As he lay in the street, he had no way of knowing a hay bale had knocked him out.

Stoker looked at the grinning face in the door of the hay loft. "Salamander Jack, is that you?"

Jack leaned out the hayloft door. "I couldn't let you just shoot him, Ranger. I owed him some misery."

"There's a fellow back behind me a ways that'll be glad he's alive. I have a few questions I want to ask him myself."

Chapter 30

"I thought that was going to be the big showdown of all showdowns," the bartender complained. "What a let-down!"

"Sorry to disappoint you," Stoker responded, "but think how bad it is for me. I ain't got to kill nobody in days."

"Hee hee hee," Jack grinned his snaggle-toothed grin. "Somebody would think you was plumb blood-thirsty was they to believe that clap-trap foolishness. I know you'd rather bring 'em in alive."

"Thanks to you I'll get the chance. Logan was fast from what I hear; I would've had no choice but to shoot to kill."

"What'd you do with him, Ranger?" the bartender asked.

"Got him handcuffed hugging the anvil over at the blacksmith's shop."

"Is that smart? A man can pick that thing up."

"If he can run for the border toting 100 pounds of anvil, more power to him. He won't be hard to run down. And I'd be tempted to just sit there and watch him try to swim the Rio Grande with it."

Jack let out with a braying laugh that sounded more like his donkey than a man. "Now I'd buy tickets to watch that."

"Yeah, I'd rather have me a good anvil than a jail

any day. I've seen men bust out of jail."

"What is that racket?" Salamander Jack headed for the front. He looked out over the batwing doors. "It's some pilgrims in a wagon. I'll be. It looks like some kind of preacher doing the driving."

The bartender scowled. "Just what I need, some Bible-thumper driving away what little bit of business that I have."

Stoker drained his glass. "Life is hard, my friend."

"So I've heard, maybe he'll be some denomination that don't mind a little libation now and then. I know when I was back

East—"

He looked up as he talked, but Stoker had turned to go to the front door.

"Yeah, right, it's okay. I talk to myself a lot in here. I'm the best company I know."

The wagons pulled up by the stable. Salamander Jack stood hat in hand as he helped the ladies down and started getting acquainted with them. Herbert unhitched the team and led them over to the corral. It looked like old home week.

A shot sounded.

Stoker drew and ran into the stable, followed closely by the others. Sam stood over Logan's body, smoking rifle in his hand. He worked the lever with difficulty; unsteady on his feet.

"Drop the gun, boy." Stoker covered him with his Colt.

"I aim to kill him, Ranger."

"You haven't already done it?" Stoker took his eyes off Sam for no more than a couple of seconds, looking for himself.

"No, he hasn't already done it." Logan raised up

his head. "You just going to stand there, or are you going to shoot him? He's wanted as much as I am."

Sam was trying to compose himself. "I was too unsteady, I missed him. I nearly got his horse though."

"Put it down, you don't want to do this."

"Oh, but I do want to do this." He brought the barrel of the rifle back up. "More than I've ever wanted to do anything in my life."

"Okay, poor choice of words, so you do want to do it, but it's not the right play."

Stoker had Sam in his sights, but he could also see Candace reminding him of his promise to her with her eyes.

"If you shoot him, it's murder. If I take him back and a jury has him hung, it'll be retribution."

"Retribution for other crimes; I want him to die for what he did to my mother."

"If you shoot him, you'll be the one to pay for that. You need him alive, son."

"He ain't gonna confess, and you're going to take me back regardless."

"Logan," the ranger said, "you listening to this? You better come clean before this boy gets steady enough to shoot you full of holes."

"How stupid do you think I am? If I confess then he has nothing to lose by doing it. Right now he needs me."

Stoker transferred his attention again. "He needs you? You saying you did it?"

"Of course I'm not saying I did it, but if he thinks I did, then he'd better keep me alive long enough to find out one way or the other, hadn't he?"

"You better quit trying my patience or I'm likely to shoot you myself."

Stoker looked back at Sam. "What is it you told me were the last words your mother said to you?"

"She said to let the law handle it."

"That's still good advice, Sam."

"I've already tried that once."

Candace walked past him and right up to Sam before anybody could make a move. She calmly took the rifle out of his hands and tossed it to Stoker.

"You men just talk a thing to death."

She put Sam's arm over her shoulders and started helping him back to the wagon. Herbert rushed to help.

"Maybe we ought to start recruiting women as rangers," Stoker said.

Peggy laughed. "Maybe you should."

<><

"Why would you want to make such a long trip?" Stoker didn't understand the old trapper. "You can't testify to anything that'd make any kind of difference."

He pulled his cinch strap tight and looped it in to secure it.

"Let's just say I'm the curious type." Jack grinned. "I always have been, not to mention the fact that you can use my help taking him back."

"The whole party is going back, I'll have help. Besides, I've never needed any help getting a prisoner back."

"Being able to do it and being able to do it easier ain't the same thing and you know it. I don't figure a preacher to be much help, and the women will be too busy fussing over Sam."

"Herbert wasn't always a preacher; his story would surprise you. I got no objection to you coming and lending a hand though." Stoker swung up into the saddle.

"Good thing 'cause I figured to do it regardless. I was the one that caught him, after all."

"You were, and now that I think on it, there may be a reward for that."

"No fooling? You mean I been knocking myself out all these years trapping animals to get their hides and I could have made more money tracking people?"

"Ain't that a kick in the head?"

"Well, I'm too long in the tooth to start taking up a new career." Jack swung up into the saddle. "Good to have my horse back."

"Where's your donkey?"

"I gave him to this Mexican family on the edge of town.

They've got a couple of short-legged kids. He won't have to do nothing harder than toting those kids around and maybe carrying a little firewood. He seems to enjoy the company."

Stoker smiled a rare smile. "Good for you."

They could hear the wagon creaking onto the road ahead of them. Jack looked at the wagon and said, "Whatcha gonna to do about the boy?"

"I don't mind admitting that frets me. If we can't get a confession out of Logan, best I can do is go back and speak for Sam."

"What good would that do, ain't he already been tried?"

"Yes, I couldn't change that, but I know the governor; I could talk to him."

"He likely to do anything?"

"I seriously doubt it, but I'd have to give it a shot."

"You can't just let him go?"

185

"I've never turned my back on the law; I don't know that I could bring myself to do it now."

"Well, we best get your boy afore they run off and leave us."

Stoker rode over to take the lead on the outlaw's horse from Sheriff Monahan. Logan had leg irons on clamping his legs underneath the horse's belly. His hands were manacled together and to the saddle-horn.

"This galoot is trussed up like a Christmas turkey. He ain't going nowhere."

Jack cackled. "Well, nowhere that old horse ain't going anyway. You sure that animal is gonna make it all the way back? That old donkey is in better shape than that thing."

"He'll make it fine," Stoker said. "We're not going to be pushing him any. Besides," Stoker gave the old trapper a sly grin, "should he break away from us, I don't figure him to be hard to run down, do you?"

Jack cackled even louder. "Now you said a whole mouthful there, Ranger, a whole mouthful. You don't take chances with a prisoner, do you?"

"That's why I always bring them back; I don't give them any opportunity to make me shoot 'em."

Chapter 31

"They have to believe you now," Candace said.

The young couple was having the same discussion back in the wagon that Stoker and Salamander Jack were having riding back behind them, but reaching different conclusions.

"I sure hope you're right."

"Of course I'm right, you'll see. I can testify that Logan actually admitted it to me. They can see for themselves that he matches the description you gave way back when it happened. Ranger Stoker is ready to speak for you, and I do think they'll get the truth out of Logan. Don't you think so, Reverend Green?"

Herbert looked over his shoulder inside the wagon. "Don't I think what?"

"Don't you think they'll get the truth out of Logan and clear Sam?"

"Logan is an extremely stubborn man, without an ounce of charity in his soul. But on the other hand, Jacob is an honorable man and he will do his utmost to see Sam cleared."

Peggy leaned back inside to add, "Don't you fret, dear, trust Jacob. He'll see that justice is done."

Sam didn't look convinced, but everyone else seemed to be, or else they were just trying to relieve his mind. "I sure hope you're right, Preacher."

<>

As the days wore on, their optimism began to fade. The entire group worked on Logan day and night, but the more they pressured him, the more set in his ways he seemed to get.

"It ain't ever going to happen," Stoker said. "He's going to take the truth to his grave just to spite us."

"That's the meanest man I ever saw," Candace said.

"There has to be some other way," Sam said.

They sat around the fire chewing it over. In spite of the points Candace made, the facts were that there were no witnesses and the only evidence available seemed to point directly at Sam. The more they gnawed on it, the more it came up the same; they needed Logan to confess.

He enjoyed their discomfort immensely, sitting over at the side watching the drama play out, his chest heaving with silent laughter.

"Much as I'm enjoying this," he finally announced, "I'm just going to have to go answer nature's call."

He held out his hands to Stoker. "You gonna take these off? Man can't do his business proper if he can't get his hands back behind him to wipe."

Stoker got up. "You watch your language in front of these ladies."

"They too delicate to know about bodily functions?" He tipped his hat to Candace and Peggy. "Pardon, ladies, I didn't mean to talk about wiping my behind in front of you."

"Keep it up," Stoker said. "I just said I was taking

you back, I didn't promise what condition you might be in when you got there."

He pulled the key from his pocket. Logan held out his hands again.

Stoker unlocked his right leg iron, then his left hand. A mischievous smile crossed the ranger's face, then in one quick jerk he pulled Logan forward and snapped the hand and leg manacles together.

"What the —"

That ought to keep you out of trouble."

Stoker's small smile blossomed into a grin. Logan was bent over at the waist. "Ought to put you in the perfect position to do what you need to do, too."

Logan hobbled over to his saddlebags, cursing under his breath. He rummaged inside and came out with the half-used Bible. He tore some pages from it and started hobbling into the brush.

Stoker didn't believe what he was seeing. A look of pure disgust passed over the ranger's face.

"I can't believe a man would rip pages out of the Holy Book to use for toilet paper."

Logan smirked. "It's just paper to me."

"Wait a minute." Sam sat up. "I know that Bible. That belonged to my mother. You worthless—"

Sam came up from the ground leaping for the outlaw. Logan sidestepped him easily and brought his manacled hands together like a club on the back of Sam's neck. Sam went down in a heap.

Candace rushed to him. Stoker looked down at the dazed man. "Son, you ain't ever gonna get well if you don't quit getting yourself hit in the head."

Stoker looked back over at the outlaw. "Can you prove that, Sam? Can you prove that's yore mama's Bible?"

Sam sat up groggily, supported by Candace. He rubbed the back of his neck. "She recorded family births and deaths on the blank pages in it."

Stoker stepped over to get the ill-used book. He opened it gently. "Most of the front is gone, anything your mama writ here is long gone."

"Oh no," tears came into Candace's eyes.

Sam just smiled a little half smile. "We got lots of kin, Ranger. Mama used up the front a long time ago. If you'll look back in the back, you'll see where my cousin Luke got himself borned and Uncle Wilbur got himself hitched to a mail-order bride. That's where you'll find daddy's death writ down, though I reckon that one might be a bit tear stained. If I could have found it, mama's name would be right there beside him."

"Well I'll be; it's here all right."

Stoker looked over at the bush that hid his charge. "This ties it to your tail, Logan. I don't need your confession any more."

The outlaw's head bobbed as he finished his chore behind the bush. "It's just as well," he said as he hobbled back. "I was kinda getting bored with that game anyway."

Herbert shook his head slowly.

"What's the matter, Preacher?" Logan said. "Do I offend your delicate sensibilities too?"

"No, it's not that; I've seen the Lord work in some mighty mysterious ways, but I've never seen him take such a direct hand in righting a wrong."

Chapter 32

Logan was shackled to a tree outside of the main camp area. Those in the party couldn't even stand to have him around, but Herbert was sitting on a stump next to him, Bible in hand, talking with a most sincere look on his face.

Stoker looked curious. "What's going on out there?

Peggy smiled. "Herbert is bound and determined to reach him before he gets back to face what's waiting for him. My guess is Logan is going to hear a lot of it."

Stoker shook his head. "He'd have better luck trying to convert the Devil himself."

"It's never too late, Jacob, never too late."

"Well, a man sure ought to make peace with his Maker before he goes to meet him. I wish the preacher luck – got my doubts, but I wish him luck." He looked around. "Where are the young folks?"

She gestured with her head. "Sitting over by the stream."

"The boy does seem to be getting along better." He grinned. "Now that people have quit hitting him in the head every fifteen minutes."

"I'm sure that helps. He has a lot of recovering to do but it does help that he is easier in his mind. He doesn't have anything to worry about now, right?"

"It'll be all right. I'm sure we can get that judge to

set aside the conviction, and if we can't get that done with the Bible as evidence, I can get the governor to do it. I told him that."

She smiled. "Then I think I know what they might be talking about out there."

◇

Candace put a blanket over Sam's shoulders. She touched his face softly. "The scab where you were shot is healing nicely, but you have quite a bruise from where you were hit by the rifle stock."

He laughed. "I got a pretty nice lump back here where I got hit that last time, too. I have to admit I'm getting a little tired of being a punching bag."

She sat down beside him as he put the blanket and his arm over her shoulder. "That's all behind us. You have nothing to do now but get well."

"How could I not with two women fussing over me night and day?"

They sat in silence for a while. Sam could see she had something on her mind and he waited her out. He had an idea what it might be.

Finally, she looked at him shyly and said, "You told me you couldn't talk about the future or even think about it with this mess hanging over your head…"

"I thought that might be what you were thinking about. That is what I said."

"And now?"

"Well . . . I reckon it isn't cut and dried, but the Ranger thinks it's going to be all right."

"What do you think?"

"I feel pretty good about it."

192

"And?"

"And I asked Reverend Green IF I were to ask you to marry me and IF you said yes, would he go and marry us?"

She pulled away from him, surprise on her face. "Oh you did? That's rather presumptuous, going from not even talking about the future to planning it without even talking to me?"

He pulled her back to him. "Don't get all hot and bothered; I just wanted to get the lay of the land before I talked to you about it."

"And what did he say?"

"He said it was a really bad idea. He said with all this stuff so fresh on everybody's mind that if we showed up back there already married that it wouldn't sit well, particularly with your pa."

"He's right about that, Daddy would have a fit."

"He said I needed to go back and get things put to rest, then court you a little and go hat in hand to your pa and ask his permission."

She nestled under his arm. "A girl likes to be courted … and fathers like to be asked for their blessing."

They sat there cuddling for a while before she said softly, "What about Sharon?"

He feigned ignorance, "Sharon who?"

She swatted him gently on the leg. "You know who, you silly."

"You told the truth of it when you said she was all show and no go – that you were the one that was always there for me. Dunno why I didn't see it earlier."

"She isn't going to like us courting."

"She'll get used to it."

"Hello the camp!"

She looked back over his shoulder. "Who's that?"

He didn't need to look. "Salamander Jack."

"Yes, I see him, and it looks like he has a couple of rabbits."

"Ahhh, those ought to fatten that stew up nicely that Mrs. Green has on the fire."

<>

When Herbert went back to his wagon, Stoker went over to check on his prisoner.

"Look here, Ranger, keeping me shackled is one thing, but torturing me is something else."

"Torturing you? I ain't laid a hand on you."

"You know what I'm talking about. Letting that holy-roller harp at me night and day. Can't you do something about that?"

"He just wants to help you make peace with your Maker while you still can."

"I don't have no 'Maker' as you put it. There ain't no such thing as God. That's just a story that these religious people made up to make people tow the line."

Stoker picked up a stick and started doodling in the dirt with it. "You pretty sure about that?"

"Oh yeah, I'm sure."

"So you're a gambling man?"

"I do okay at the tables."

"What you're talking about is a pretty big bet. The way I see it, if you're right then those of us who believe in God have lived the best we know how for no reason. But if you're wrong, eternity is a long time to pay for a bad decision."

He snapped the twig in half as if to punctuate his

words.

"That does put a different slant on it." Logan gave Stoker a curious look. "I didn't know you were one of them believers, too. I wouldn't have taken you for one of them nuts."

"Well, I am, ever since I was a tadpole, I just don't talk about it much."

"Well, I still think … "

Chapter 33

Sheriff Fancher turned the key in the lock. He grinned at Sam. "Guess you like looking through the bars better from this side."

"That's a fact." He looked over at the outlaw in the cell. "Logan, I'd go slow laying down on that cot, there's a wire in it that'll stick you if you don't kinda ease onto it."

"Very funny," Logan said.

Sam and the sheriff turned to go into the office. Sam shrugged, "I wasn't trying to be funny."

Back behind them they heard, "Owww!"

Sam smiled. "I told you I wasn't trying to be funny."

Candace was waiting on him as he came out of the cell block. He walked over and took her hands in his. "I owe this all to you."

"Stoker is the one that found your man."

"He just did his job. You're the one who got me through this, one step at a time. I guess you've always been there for me, I just couldn't see it."

"So what do you do now?"

He smiled. "I got to go out and get the place straightened up, try to get my life going again. That's what my Mama would have wanted me to do."

"And then?"

"Like the preacher said, I reckon then I come

courting."

"You're planning to come courting?" Sharon came in the door.

Sam smiled at her but didn't let go of Candace's hands. "I plan to court the prettiest girl in town."

Sharon's face lit up. "Aren't you taking a lot for granted? I might not even want you to come calling. That line is pretty long."

"Oh, I'm sorry; you thought I was talking about you? To me Candace is the prettiest girl in town, or in the county, the state, the whole world for that matter."

"Candace?" The tone of her voice clearly said she couldn't believe what Sam had just said. She expected him to still be captivated by her. She looked at Sam. "Is this true?"

His smile lit up his face. "Yes, isn't it great?"

"Are you sure? I mean, I thought that you and I . . ."

"There is no you and I, Sharon. We're just friends the way we have always been."

She frowned. "When you were in trouble, I came after you."

"You went on an adventure, and I know I was just one cowboy out of a hundred. Candace cared, she's always cared; I just couldn't see her. The only reason you're upset is because you can't bear the idea of anybody choosing her over you. You don't want me; you just don't want her to have me."

Sharon was indignant. "That's not true."

"Yes, I'm afraid it is, but I hope we can continue to be friends."

"Friends!" she said in a shrill voice. "Oh, you!" She turned on her heel and flounced out the door.

He smirked. "I take it that's a no?"

197

Candace took his arm. "She'll get over it."

Herbert came up beside them. "Pride can be really hard to get around, but you're right, she'll get past it." He smiled at them. "In fact, I think the day is coming very soon when instead of the way it has always been … that you're going to find she's jealous of you."

◇

Stoker found the judge sitting outside the general store, sober for once. "Judge, we need to talk."

The judge gestured to the chair next to him. "Have a seat, Ranger, I have been wanting to compliment you on returning with the prisoner. I'm not sure who else you brought in but you apparently were able to resolve two cases at once."

"No, it's all the same case."

The judge looked confused. "The boy has been tried and sentenced."

"By a bunch of drunks. I know for a fact that this town has got a lot of ranchers and storekeepers . . . good people. Even your sheriff admits that trial was a farce."

The judge was indignant. "I don't agree."

Stoker reached into his saddlebag and pulled out the desecrated

Bible. "I took this off the prisoner that I've got in your jail. He was using it for toilet paper."

"Who would do such a thing?"

"Exactly. The long and the short of it is that it is Mrs. Duncan's Bible. All the family history in the front is all torn out, but there is plenty left in the back to put a noose around Logan's neck."

"Logan?"

198

"The man with the marled eye that the boy tried to tell you about but you wouldn't listen."

The judge paled, sure he was watching his re-election chances slipping rapidly away. "I didn't know."

"Of course you didn't." Stoker took the Bible back. "The way I see it you have two choices. You convene court immediately and set that conviction aside, or I go to the governor, who is a friend of mine, and I get him to do it. If I have to go that route you're going to be the laughing stock of the entire area."

The judge cleared his throat. "Yes, well of course I have to see that justice is done. I'll see to it immediately."

"Now, about the trial for the real killer."

"Yes, yes, I'll get that set up immediately."

"Actually, because of the legal situation in this little town, I telegraphed the governor and he's sending a circuit-riding judge over here to conduct the trial.

"I don't see that as being necessary."

"I'm sure you don't. I'm sure you figure your reputation has taken a hit over the wrongful conviction of Sam, and I'm betting you're thinking this other trial could repair the damage."

"I was thinking no such thing."

"Whether it's true or not, it's already set up."

"You can't talk to me like that."

Stoker got right in Larribee's face. "You're a minor city official; I'm a duly constituted state official. You don't want to go head to head with me on this."

The judge's indignation faded. If he didn't play his cards right, he could be through around here and the ranger had made it clear that he was just the man to do it.

"Don't worry, Judge. You'll still get your chance to redeem yourself. Having a different presiding judge will mean there are two lawyers in town. You two are finally going to get to square off against each other head to head."

Chapter 34

The stage pulled into Turkey Creek and a distinguished gentleman with silver hair and a matching mustache and goatee stepped down to survey the street. His name was Clarence Farnsworth, a name well known in legal circles.

Semi-retired after a long and distinguished career that had culminated in his serving as a Federal judge, he now took occasional cases that interested him serving at the governor's pleasure.

This case interested him, not so much for the particulars of the case but for the way he had been told justice seemed to be dispensed in this little town. He would insure that it would be conducted properly. He had never had a decision reversed on him, and had no intention of starting now.

From the restaurant in the front of the boarding house, Judge Larribee and lawyer Eggleston watched him arrive. Eggleston saw him first. "That's got to be him."

Larribee nodded. "Yes, he has the look.

As they watched, Stoker came over to meet him, and Judge Farnsworth put a hand on the big man's shoulder as they shook hands. It was clear they were friends. Eggleston said, "Uh-oh."

"Indeed. We had better play our cards right in this or both of us may be hunting a new place to call home."

"Speak for yourself. Even if nobody wants me for a lawyer, I still have a thriving business as a barber."

The truth of what Eggleston said was suddenly blazingly clear to the little judge. All of the years that he had spent ridiculing Eggleston's other profession took on a different meaning right in front of his eyes. He had something to fall back on. Larribee's heart sank as he realized he had absolutely nothing to fall back on.

Larribee said as much. "After all these years of making fun of it, I find myself envious of your barber shop."

Eggleston grinned. What a red-letter day! Regardless how this came out, this was the ultimate victory over his old friend.

Friend? Was Larribee a friend? Years of squabbling and fighting, how would he feel if he watched the man ride off, leaving town for good. He would miss him terribly.

"What's the matter? You look like you just lost your last friend."

Eggleston shook his head slowly. "No, but if I'm not careful I might do just that."

Larribee didn't get it. "What are you talking about?"

"Don't you see? After the years of fussing and fighting, it just dawned on me how I would feel if you left town for good. I was stunned to realize that you are my best friend."

"Best friend?" Larribee laughed a belly laugh. "Don't be ridiculous. Why we haven't gotten along a single day that we have known each other."

"But would you miss it? Who would take my

place?"

The laughter faded from Larribee's face. "I guess I would miss it. I never thought about it, but our confrontations are what makes life bearable in this little town. Friends. It never occurred to me."

"It doesn't mean we should quit competing with each other, but it sure puts a different face on it."

"That it does."

◇

"Jacob Stoker, it's good to see you."

The judge put his hand on Stoker's shoulder as they shook hands. Stoker smiled. "Judge Farnsworth, if they had let me choose who to come handle this mess, you would be the man I would have thought of."

"I appreciate that. What is your role here?"

"I just brought in the accused, Sir. He may be a handful to handle so I figured to stay around to make sure nothing went wrong before the process is done. That and the fact that I'm pretty sure I'll be called to testify."

They release hands and the judge said, "Commendable, and the ultimate professional peace officer as usual. I won't ask you what your opinion is on the guilt or innocence of the accused."

"I wouldn't say if you did. Ain't my job to try them, just to bring them to trial."

"Precisely what I would expect you to say." He looked up and down the street. "I fail to discern a courthouse in this small town."

"No, Sir, there isn't one. The only place large enough for a trial is the saloon."

"Very well, certainly not the first time I have had to do that. Are there lawyers available?"

"There's one, and the town judge. I don't want to tell you your business but I figured with you here it would free him up to handle the other side."

"I think that would work admirably. Anything else I should know?"

"Just that I'm pretty sure the town judge is an alcoholic. He has been staying sober the past few days. Did you hear about the last trial he presided over?"

"Yes, I was briefed on that. You may be assured that it will go differently this time."

"I have no doubt of that." Stoker looked at the two men approaching. "It appears you are about to meet the entire Turkey Creek legal profession all at one time."

The two men walked up, and Stoker made the introductions.

"Judge Farnsworth," Larribee said. "I'm honored to meet you, Sir. Your name is well known to everyone in the legal profession."

Farnsworth laughed. "Judge Larribee, it may be even better known around the various penal institutions in the state."

They all joined him in the laughter. Eggleston took his turn to shake his hand. "I am honored to meet you as well."

"Let me commend you gentlemen for managing to fashion a degree of justice under difficult circumstances. I know it has to be rather cobbled together in some circumstances but I am sure you have done your best regardless of the outcome of this last trial."

Larribee looked like he had swallowed a frog. "Yes, well…"

Judge Farnsworth held up a hand to stop him.

"Water under the bridge. We have all made our mistakes. But let me ask you about the decorum that I may expect in the conduct of this trial. I am given to understand that there is bad blood between the two of you?"

Eggleston said, "If you had asked me that even a couple of days ago, I would have said yes. However, we have come to understand that the competition between us is what we thrive on.

"I might add that we have been rather startled to find out that we are actually best friends."

The Judge threw his head back and laughed. "Oh, that is just excellent. Good natured competition is what makes the justice system work, gentlemen, and I am most pleased to find out that is exactly what I may expect."

The judge looked around. "Very well, let us make our way over to the so-called courtroom. I have to break the bad news to the proprietor that he is, as of right now, closed for business so that we may set up for the trial."

He smiled. "And so we will have a town full of clear headed men tomorrow when it begins."

Chapter 35

Judge Farnsworth knew his business. He had Sheriff Fancher send riders out to the ranches for solid men who hopefully didn't know as much about the events that had transpired as people in town. He wanted the most objective jury pool that he could get. Of course, the word went out around town as well.

Then he went about setting up the courtroom. He started by putting twelve chairs with their backs up against the bar to reduce the chances that anyone might be preoccupied by wishing it was open. But he knew if he got the right men on the jury that it would not be a problem anyway.

The judge's bench would be a table against the back wall at right angles to the jury box with a witness chair next to it. Two tables with chairs were set up for the prosecution and defense. The remainder of the room was set up with all of the chairs that were left. In anticipation of an overflow crowd, Reverend Green had provided benches that he used in his camp meetings for additional seating.

He looked around, satisfied that it was the best he could do under the circumstances. He turned his attention to the two lawyers. "Very well, gentlemen, do you approve?"

They both murmured that it was better than it had ever been done. "Trappings are important, gentlemen.

It helps set the tone for what we hope will be a good trial. Now, as to the roles that you will play. Mr. Eggleston, I know the county will pay you to be the prosecutor, and Judge Larribee, you continue to be paid whether you are presiding or not, so the court is going to appoint you to act for the defense. Regardless of your personal opinion, I expect you to give the accused the best defense you can devise."

Larribee looked sour. "This isn't going to sit well with the town-folks, me standing up for him."

"I understand that and I will make it quite clear in the trial why you are doing it, but the man is entitled to the best defense that we can give him."

"Yes, Sir."

<>

Judge Farnsworth had said that trappings set the tone for the trial and he meant it. As instructed, Sheriff Fancher got the overflow crowd's attention, then said "Please rise for the Honorable Judge Clarence Farnsworth."

The judge came out of the storage room in a black judicial robe. The man knew how to set the stage.

Arriving at his bench, he said, "You may be seated."

The crowd settled themselves in. The judge looked out over them. "We have before us a serious matter today. I want it well understood that regardless of any feelings that you may have about this case, I have instructed Judge Larribee that he is to give the defendant the best defense he is capable of giving.

"If you have feelings about the defendant, you will not hold that against the judge, he will be doing his duty. Having said that, it is the last time I will use the title judge in connection with him. He is entitled to such recognition whether he is presiding or not, but to prevent confusion during the course of the trial, he will simply be Mr. Larribee or lawyer Larribee. There is no slight intended, but just for the duration of the trial, it will simplify things."

Larribee stood. "I understand, Your Honor, and there is no offense taken."

"Very well, Mr. Larribee, how does your client plead?"

"He pleads not guilty, Your Honor."

A loud murmuring erupted from those assembled but the judge gaveled them to silence. "During the course of the trial, the reaction of the spectators will be subdued or I will clear the courtroom, is that understood? I would hope regardless of what all of you feel or think, you might know that you will listen to all of the evidence before you make up your mind. This is particularly important since our jury is still sitting out there among you."

He turned to the sheriff. "Sheriff Fancher, proceed with the jury selection."

Speaking to the crowd he said, "According to the law in this county, it is necessary to be a property owner in order to be a registered voter. The sheriff has the names of all of those who qualify on slips of paper in this box. As your name is called, please come up and take a seat in the jury box. The lawyers will then ask questions and challenge the jurors. If a juror is disqualified for cause, the same process will be used to replace them until we have a panel of twelve."

The jury took their seats and the lawyers began to question them. They accepted five jurors, mostly from outlying ranches before they got down to the storekeeper Ray Bates.

Larribee said, "Ray, I have to think you are pretty close to this case, and your daughter is slated to testify. Do you think you can keep an open mind and listen to the evidence?"

The storekeeper thought on it briefly and said, "In all honesty, no, I don't believe I can be objective about it. It isn't in me to not believe my daughter on this."

The judge said, "Thank you for your honesty, Mr. Bates, you are excused."

He looked at the remainder of the unchallenged jurors. "As long as we are at it, is there anyone else who feels they cannot be objective on this case?"

Colonel Delmar raised his hand. "I'm afraid I feel the same as Ray on this, Your Honor, and for the same reason. Different daughter, but the same reason."

The judge excused him. One other rancher was also excused, a neighbor of the victim who said he was simply too close to her to be fair in his opinion of the case. They were replaced and the jury settled in at twelve.

The judge looked at Eggleston and said, "Mr. Prosecutor, your opening remarks."

Eggleston walked around the table where he could easily be seen by both the jury and the crowd. He was no strutting bird this time. This was more of a trial than he had ever participated in.

"Your Honor, members of the jury," he began, "we are here today to assess the guilt or innocence of the defendant," he pointed, "Rafe Logan, on the charge that he did murder Shirley Duncan with malice aforethought. We believe that the evidence that we intend to present will prove that charge beyond a reasonable doubt."

"Thank you," the judge turned to Larribee. "Counsel for the defense."

Larribee moved around the table perhaps aware that he had as much on the line as did the man he was representing. "Your Honor, members of the jury, the prosecutor is correct, we are here to assess the guilt or innocence of my client. However, we believe the evidence is going to show that there are no witnesses to this crime, and the case of the prosecution is going to rest on the fact that the defendant simply had possession of the woman's Bible.

"He freely admits that but maintains that he found the Bible lying by the road. While I disapprove in the strongest of terms the purpose for which he wanted to take the Bible with him, it does not prove it was he who committed this act.

"We believe the jury will have no choice but to conclude based on the evidence that there is a reasonable doubt, and in such a case the defendant must be acquitted."

"Thank you. Mr. Prosecutor, you may begin to present your case."

<>

Eggleston took a deep breath and expelled it slowly. He hadn't anticipated the 'I just found the Bible' defense, and he should have. He had his work cut out for him.

"The prosecution calls Samuel Duncan."

Sam was sworn in and Eggleston moved in front of him. "Mr. Duncan, can you tell us in your own words what happened at your house?"

Sam tensed. He had had time to come to terms with his mother's death but the way he tensed up clearly said it was still difficult for him to think about it.

The prosecutor saw this and said, "Take your time, Mr. Duncan, I know this is difficult for you."

"I rode all night from where I was working to get home, and when I got there I found my mother dying on the floor. She told me a man with a marled eye tried to attack her and she had fought him off, marking him with her knife before he stabbed her with it."

"Objection. Hearsay," Larribee said. "There are no witnesses to that."

"Over-ruled," the judge said. "There is a witness, and he is testifying. The jury is entitled to place whatever value upon the statement that they wish. As with every witness that comes up here, that is the major part of the job of the jury, to determine whether something is true or not when they hear it."

Good, Eggleston thought, but what is my opponent about to do to counter that? Sam's trial, that's what. He had to move to defuse that before Larribee did it.

"Mr. Duncan, did the law initially believe that it was done by this mysterious man?"

"No, people didn't believe me."

"Didn't they, in fact, accuse you of the murder, even go so far as to convict you of it?"

"Yes."

"What changed?"

"A Texas Ranger by the name of Jacob Stoker come up with stuff that caused the judge to set aside the conviction because he could see I didn't do it."

"Is the person that set aside that conviction here in the room?"

Sam pointed. "The judge done it." He looked up at the bench. "I'm sorry; I guess I'm supposed to say Mr. Larribee done it."

"One more thing, Mr. Duncan. Did the defendant actually admit to you that he murdered your mother?"

"Yes, he did."

"Why would he do such a thing?"

"He was about to kill me. He never thought I'd be able to testify."

"Were there any witnesses to this?"

"One, Candace Bates. She heard him."

"Why would he allow that?

"He planned on killing her, too, when he got through with her."

An uproar erupted in the courtroom, and the judge had to gavel them again to silence. "I warned you about that, there will be no demonstrations in here or I will clear the courtroom."

"One last thing, were you the one who identified your mother's Bible?"

"I was, but I didn't have to be, the things she had written in the back spelled it out clearly enough."

"Pass the witness."

<>

Larribee shook his head. He had underestimated his old friend. He was sure he had blindsided him with the 'just found the Bible' defense, but Eggleston in turn had pulled his teeth by pointing out he had been the one to set aside the earlier conviction. He sighed. Best to try to salvage what he could with the witness.

He walked over to the witness chair. "Mr. Duncan, do you know what it means that our law protects us from double jeopardy?"

"No."

"It means a man can't be tried for the same crime twice. That means you could just sit here and admit that you did it and we couldn't do a thing about it."

"Why on earth would I do that when I didn't do it?"

"To clear your conscience. Just like I have to clear mine when I sit here and think I might have been premature in setting aside that conviction. I should at least have had a re-trial.

"But that is water under the bridge." He didn't want to go any further with that. Maybe he cast a little doubt, maybe he didn't but any more and he'd get a face-full of rebuttal and that he didn't want. "Let's turn to the Bible in question. You made it very clear that it was your mother's Bible, but how can you prove that he took it instead of finding it by the road as he says?"

"Common sense, I guess. Why would someone bother to take it and then just throw it away?"

Whoops, that didn't go as well as I planned. "Why indeed? I guess we'll never know."

He turned to the judge. "That's all I have for this witness."

<>

Eggleston stood. "The prosecution calls Miss Candace Bates."

She was sworn in and he moved over to her. "Miss Bates, you seem to have been very involved in this from the beginning, why is that?"

He was well aware of the line of counterattack for her testimony and again wanted to defuse it if he could.

She was wide-eyed and nervous. "I saw Sam as soon as he was brought in and have been in contact with him throughout the whole ordeal."

"So you are friends?"

"Yes."

"Good friends?"

"Yes."

He leaned over close to her. "More than friends?"

She reddened and in a small voice said, "Yes."

"Miss Bates, do you love him?"

An even smaller reply, "Yes."

The judge said, "Miss Bates, you are going to have to speak up where the jury can hear you."

She lifted her chin defiantly. "Yes, it is true that I love him."

"I see, if that is the case, would you lie for him?"

"I would, but I'm not. He has already been tried and released and is in no danger, so I have no reason to lie."

Perfect, he thought. I couldn't have planned that out better myself. "Miss Bates, did you hear the defendant admit to killing the victim?"

"Yes, but he said if I told anybody that they would just think I was covering for Sam. I'm not."

"One last question, Miss Bates, were you ever in fear for your life from this man?"

"Very much so. I had no doubt that after he killed Sam, he would have his way with me and then dispose of me as well. He is the most evil person I have ever met."

"Pass the witness."

◇

Larribee sat looking at her. Eggleston had put him in a box.

Anything he said was just likely to nail her points down more. He only saw one course of action.

"I have no need to put Miss Bates through any further torment, Your Honor. She has already admitted that she would be willing to lie for Mr. Duncan and that would be all that I would be trying to ascertain from her."

The judge was unable to completely suppress a small smile. "The witness may step down. I believe I will call a recess for lunch. Everyone be back in your places by one o'clock."

He banged down the gavel.

Chapter 36

In the residence behind the general store, Ray Bates, Candace, Sharon and Sam were eating a quick lunch.

Ray looked over at Sam and said, "So how do you think it is going?"

Sam shook his head. "At the last trial, most of the time I didn't have a clue as to what was going on. This time ain't much better. What do you think?"

"I think both of you youngsters did a fine job testifying." He took his daughter's hand and added, "I'm very proud of you."

He thought on it a moment more. "Overall, I think both sides have made some solid points. It looks to me like it is going to come down to whether the jury thinks a reasonable doubt exists or not."

Sam frowned. "I just don't understand this reasonable doubt business."

"What it boils down to is whether the jury can feel absolutely certain in their verdict or even if they do believe a certain way is there any reason that they can't be completely sure."

"That sounds like a pretty big fence to have to jump over."

"Our system of justice is weighted in favor of the defendant. That didn't help you in your first trial, though, did it?"

"It sure didn't."

"Well, there's one thing bothering me," Sharon said. "I don't understand why I'm not being called to testify."

Sam said, "Yeah, I wondered about that."

Ray knew she couldn't stand being left out of the spotlight. He said, "What do you feel you know that should be brought out in the trial?"

"I know that horrible man did it."

"And just how do you know that? What proof could you offer? If you have something or heard him admit something we could make sure the prosecutor knew it."

She pouted. "All right, I admit it; I just don't like being left out."

<>

The judge gaveled the trial back to order and Eggleston immediately called Sergeant Jake Stoker of the Texas Rangers to the stand. The oath was administered and the prosecutor moved to question him.

"Ranger, let me first commend you on the fine job you did of bringing both men back to justice and the strong role you played in getting Mr. Duncan's conviction set aside."

"I didn't do anything but my duty. That's what I do, I bring men in and I bring what evidence I can find along with them. What the court does with it ain't up to me."

"Still, you were very steadfast in your duty. Now let me ask you, how did you come to bring in two men? You just left on the trail of one, isn't that true?"

"Yes and no." He shifted in his seat as if he were trying to frame the words. "Officially, I was just after Duncan, but the sheriff let me know that he thought the possibility of there being another suspect had been completely ignored in the trial. He didn't ask anything more of me other than for me to keep an open mind on the possibility.

"When I got down the road and found that a man of that exact description had robbed a bank in Millers Run, I got more than curious."

"Did you ever hear the defendant come right out and admit the crime?"

"No, I got him dead to rights on a half dozen other crimes from bank robbery to stagecoach holdups along with some other stuff but he just wouldn't admit that it was him that killed Mrs. Duncan."

"You were there when he was confronted with Mrs. Duncan's Bible?"

"I was."

"And he admitted to the murder at that time?"

"He did. When I said the Bible tied that murder to his tail, he said 'It is just as well because I'm getting kind of bored with that game anyway.'"

"Meaning he did it?"

"That's what it sounds like to me."

"Pass the witness."

<>

Larribee advanced on the ranger. "He was getting kind of bored with that game anyway?"

"That's what he said."

"Yes, he told me he said that, only he said he wasn't confessing, he was just telling people he was tired of all the back and forth on it and didn't intend to do it anymore."

"I guess the jury will have to decide if that's what he meant or not."

"Yes, or they could decide they just can't tell what he meant, which would constitute a reasonable doubt."

He stood and looked over at the jury before he added, "I'm through with this witness."

The judge looked at the prosecutor. "You have further witnesses to present?"

"Just one, Your Honor, the prosecution calls Reverend
Herbert Green."

The preacher was sworn and took his place in the witness chair.

"Reverend Green, first let me ask if you can confirm the testimony that has been given so far of the events that happened in your presence?"

"I can, I was there when they discovered that the Bible the defendant was carrying did indeed belong to Mrs. Duncan."

Eggleston picked the Bible up from the judge's bench. "Is this the Bible in question?"

The preacher took it and flipped it to the back. He handed it back to Eggleston. "That's it."

Eggleston held it up where the jury could easy see it as he continued. "I suppose the reason he was carrying this Bible was repugnant to you?"

"Of course it was, my entire life is centered around that book."

"Yet, even at that, you still reached out to him?"

"I did. It was important to me to try to help him reconcile with his Maker before he had to go meet him face to face." He looked over at Logan. "It still is important to me."

Logan made a pained expression and rolled his eyes.

"So you spent a lot of time talking with him about it."

"Every evening the entire trip back."

Eggleston set the Bible back on the table. "Did you feel you were making progress?"

The preacher shook his head sadly. "I fear he only got frustrated and more and more angry. He tried every which way to make me quit talking to him, but I wouldn't give up."

"Boy, you got that right," Logan said, "the man don't know how to shut up."

The judge banged his gavel. "The defendant is out of order. You will get your chance to speak if you decide to take the stand."

Eggleston framed the next question carefully. This was the big one. "Did anything come from these discussions that has a bearing on this case?"

"He was particularly mad and frustrated one night when I told him if he didn't change his ways he was going to hell. He told me that his ticket to hell was bought and paid for when he killed Sam's mom and there was nothing I could do about it."

Logan was on his feet. "This ain't right, that's just something I said to try and make him leave me alone. I didn't mean it for real."

The courtroom buzzed, and the judge had to gavel several times to restore order. "Mr. Logan, I'm not going to tell you again it is not your time to talk."

Eggleston said, "Well, that saves me from having to cross-examine him to see if he actually said that."

The gavel came down hard again. "You are out of

order, too, Mr. Prosecutor, save it for your summation."

"Pass the witness."

◇

Larribee ducked his head to talk to his client. "Why on earth didn't you tell me about that?"

Logan sneered. "I didn't figure it was important. Besides, that crazy man talked so long and hard, who could remember what he said or what I said for that matter. Put me on the stand and I'll tell them he's lying."

"Oh, that's a great strategy. Your big move is to accuse a man of the cloth with lying."

"You got a better idea?"

"No, I don't. I don't have any more ideas."

He looked up at the Reverend. There was nothing he could do in cross examination that wouldn't make it worse.
"I have no questions for this witness."

"What?" Logan snarled. "You aren't even going to try?"

"There's nothing I could ask him that wouldn't make it worse. We're going to have to go with your big move."

Behind him, he heard Eggleston say, "the prosecution rests, Your Honor."

The judge followed it up with, "Witnesses for the defense, Mr. Larribee?"

He got up reluctantly. This was against his better judgment. "Just one, Your Honor, I call the defendant, Rafe Logan."

Logan was sworn and took the stand.

Larribee didn't have any idea how to proceed so he just tossed it out. It went against every grain of his being to assist a man in what he knew was about to be a pack of lies, but he had it to do. "Mr. Logan, when did you first become aware of the murder of Mrs. Duncan?"

"When that fool ranger arrested me. That's the first I heard of it."

"Did you rob the bank in Millers Run?"

"Yeah I done that. Wish I hadn't because that put me in the cross-hairs of that Duncan looking to find somebody to blame for his ma's murder to get the blame off him."

"Did you meet him in the mountains and try to kill him?"

"Course not, what reason would I have to do that? I dunno who shot him, but he figured to use it to try and get himself off. He probably done it himself and just managed to do it worse than he planned."

"Did you hold up the stagecoach?"

"Yeah, I done that, too. I ain't hiding the fact that I tend to rob people, but I'm no murderer."

Larribee had to admit the man was sounding half-way credible so far. More than he ever expected. But the next one would be tough. "Mr. Logan, did you try to kill Mr. Duncan at the waterhole and threaten Miss Bates?"

Logan laughed. "Now that there is the biggest windy of them all. That little wench sat over there and admitted that she'd lie for him and everybody is just taking it in hook, line and sinker. He's trying to frame me for the murder and she's more than willing to go along with it."

Now for the big one. "Last question, did you

confess the murder to Reverend Green?"

"Confess a murder? I weren't doing more than confessing that I wanted to stop talking about all of it. You have no idea what it was like having that man digging at you night and day. I was ready to pull my hair out."

"You don't think he had good intentions?"

"I'm sure he did, the way he looks at that mumbo-jumbo but I just wanted him to stop."

"Pass the witness."

"I have no questions, Your Honor. I can't think of any questions that I could ask that wouldn't just produce a bunch more lies on top of the ones we just heard."

Bang! The gavel came down again. "What is it you don't understand about save it for the summation, Counselor?"

"Isn't it time for my summation?"

"Well, if the defense has no more witnesses, I suppose it is."

Larribee said, "I have no further witnesses."

"Very well, we will take a short recess and come back for your summations."

Chapter 37

"I done good, didn't I?" Logan grinned.

"Actually you managed to raise enough dust to possibly obscure the fact that you are lying through your teeth, as bad as I hate to be a party to it."

Larribee felt like he had done all he could. Now all he could do was sit back and hope the jury saw through it. It was a tricky line to have to walk to do your duty as well as you could do it but still down deep hope you would not be successful. At least he could take comfort in the fact that at no point had he himself ever lied.

But maintaining that through the summation would be a challenge indeed.

The judge gaveled it back to order.

It was time to walk that line.

Eggleston would go first and he walked over to take his place in front of the jury. "I'm impressed," he said. "What we just witnessed was some of the most sincere and accomplished lying that I have ever had the opportunity to witness. It was amazing.

"Who could believe that a man with such a checkered past could sit there and malign a man of the cloth, a Texas Ranger who has become a legend in his own lifetime, a young lady of our community that all of you know is of spotless virtue, and a young man who, although he went through a tough time, came through it all with an amazing display of character?"

Eggleston held up his hands in a gesture of surrender. "Yet he did it. He pulled it off. He managed to discount all of their testimony as a pack of lies, and I have to say sounded half-way credible about it. But I'm betting most of you have been lied to before in your lives. Don't you have a little alarm that goes off in the back of your head that tells you when somebody is piling it on thick and deep?"

He turned and looked at Logan and pointed. "This man has no character and no honor. Putting his hand on that Bible and swearing to tell the truth meant nothing to him, you saw what he thinks a Bible is worth. Why on earth would you believe a word he said?"

He turned and walked back to his table. Halfway there, he stopped and turned to say, "We proved our case. We know it, and you know it. And we did it with the testimony of some upstanding people."

<>

Wow, Larribee thought. His old friend had really risen to the occasion. He was seriously impressed and would tell him so at the first opportunity. But for right now, he had to rise to the occasion, too. Given the way he was feeling about his client, he didn't know how he was going to do it.

He walked over in front of the jury. Then he turned to face his client.

"Is he lying? Look at him. Dirty, bad manners, carved up piecemeal where he looks like he has more scars than skin. And he's an outlaw by his own admission. He is not a nice person. But guess what?

225

We aren't here to judge him for what he is or what he has done with his life. We are only here to judge whether he did that one act of violence.

"Did he murder Mrs. Duncan in cold blood? You've heard all the evidence, but there is one last thing you need to know, and I'm sure the judge will mention it in his charge to the jury, but we don't have to prove he is innocent. Let me say that again, we don't have to prove he is innocent!"

He slowly walked down the line making eye contact with them one at a time.

"We only have to raise a reasonable doubt. We only have to cause you to not be absolutely sure. Are you 100 percent positive that he did this? Is there no possibility at all that you might be wrong? If there is, you have to acquit, it's the law."

He turned and went back to his table. Did he walk the line? Did he do enough to satisfy the law? Did he do too much and actually get the man off? He scarcely heard the judge charge the jury and send them off to deliberate.

<>

The judge and both lawyers went over to the Sheriff's Office to wait. When they entered, the judge said, "Gentlemen, let me congratulate you both on a fine trial. I will admit that I was not expecting the degree of skill that I saw based on what I had heard about justice in this town."

Larribee looked over at his friend, "Roger, I cannot tell you how impressed I am with your performance. It was awesome. I have been greatly underestimating you."

"And I you, old friend. Your performance was amazing."

"I would like to ask the two of you something, but I need your word that it is not to leave this room."

They agreed.

"The man is guilty, and I think both of you know that." Both men nodded. "I was so torn between feeling like I gave him the representation he was entitled to under the law, but hoping I would not succeed. I don't know whether I actually walked that line or not."

The judge smiled. "The eternal legal question. If my opinion matters, I think you did all you could."

"But did I do too much?"

"Horace, all you can do is your best and hope that the jury gets it right. I think you did your best with what you had to work with."

"Well, there is one other thing," Judge Farnsworth said, "In my charge to the jury, I was careful to point out that the words reasonable doubt don't mean no doubt at all but mean that there couldn't be enough doubt to cause a reasonable man to question his decision."

Larribee sighed. "I hope that is enough."

"If it isn't, then the man deserves to walk."

Sheriff Fancher stuck his head in the door. "Jury is coming back."

Farnsworth looked at them. "It's the moment of truth, gentlemen. Shall we go see?"

<><

When court was back in session, the judge said, "Have you a verdict?"

One man stood up. "I reckon they choose me to say it. Judge, we just ain't buying that line of bull that big fellow over there tried to sell us. We figure he's guilty as sin."

"So say you all?"

The entire jury panel nodded.

"Then the jury is excused with our gratitude. Will the prisoner come forward for sentencing?"

Logan shuffled forward, his manacles and leg irons still in place.

The judge stood to make sure he could be heard through the whole room. "I have something to say before sentencing that I want the whole town to hear. Judge Larribee, I wish to commend you on doing a fine job of giving this man every ounce of representation the law afforded him even though I know you did not really want to do it. I don't see how you could have done more."

He looked up at the crowd. "… and I admonish this town not to hold this matter of representation against him."

He paused a moment, then decided to go further. "I also have a recommendation to make. I think you need to continue to have a municipal judge to handle the day to day legal matters in your community, but in the future, I believe it should be standard practice to bring a circuit judge in for serious matters to allow these two fine lawyers to continue to face off and see that justice is done in your community."

He sat back down. "Now, Mr. Logan, having been found guilty by a jury of your peers, it is my duty to sentence you to be transported to Territorial Prison where, at the warden's convenience, execution by hanging shall be carried out."

"Humph," Logan said. "You got to get me there first."

"I'll take care of that part of it, Judge." Stoker walked up to them. "I'll get him there, and I ain't never lost a prisoner."

Chapter 38

Sam walked into the general store. It was time.

Ray Bates looked up and worked hard to suppress the smile on his face. "Hello, Sam, something I can do for you?"

He knew why Sam was there. He could make this easy or he could have some fun out of the lad. He really wanted to do the latter, but his daughter would kill him if he did.

"Sir, I think you know why I'm here."

"Yes, I do know, and I appreciate you coming to ask for her hand. I know you could have come back home married, and waiting to do it right shows very good judgment. Still, you are both very young. Can you provide for her?"

Sam whipped his hat off and was worrying it in his hands. "I have a house, Sir, I've got it fixed up real nice."

"Yes, yes you do but it's still a house that sits on someone else's land."

"It won't always be that way. I'm a hard worker."

"I can attest to that." Both men turned to see Pop and Hattie coming in the door. Pop extended his hand to the storekeeper. "I'm Jeremiah Whitaker, but everyone calls me Pop. This here is my wife Hattie."

"Pleased to meet you. My name is Ray Bates."

"We got really fond of this young man in the short

time he was with us. I never seen such a hard worker in all my borned days."

Ray nodded. "Everybody pretty much says the same thing about him."

"We came over to see if we could do something about the scrape he had with the law, but it appears the dust has already all settled on that."

"Yes, he has been cleared of all charges."

Hattie clasped her hands together. "Oh, I am so very pleased to hear that. Is Candace here?"

"She's back in the back. But unless I miss my guess she's hiding behind that curtain waiting to see how I respond to the question this young man is asking me."

Candace came through the curtain.

Pop laughed. "It appears we have interrupted something."

Ray laughed with him. "Nothing but this young man asking for my daughter's hand. I was just grilling him on how he was going to provide for her. I haven't gotten his answer yet."

"Then perhaps it is a good thing I am here. My hired hand got to be friends with Colonel Delmar while he was at our place and, well, the Colonel hired him away from me. I heard as I walked in that all Sam had to offer was a rented place on somebody else's land. I surely would like to have him come back to our place."

"I'd like that," Sam extended his hand.

Pop took it but didn't release it. "That ain't the whole of it. We were right taken with this young lady, too."

He extended his other hand and Candace moved to take it. "The Missus and I never had no kids. No family at all really. I'm not just offering you the chance to work on the place, I'm offering you the chance to be part of our family. To inherit the ranch someday."

"Oh my, yes," Hattie said. "We would so love to see some youngsters on the place. It gladdens my heart just to think of it."

Pop took their hands and put them together as he released them. "I don't know what comes first, your pa's blessing, or you taking me up on our offer."

Ray said, "It would be hard to see her move away, she's all I have. But if Sam is going to be fixed that well, I have to give my blessing."

Pop smiled. "Don't worry, it's not that long a ride, particularly if you're coming to see your grandkids."

Sam said, "That road runs both ways, we won't be strangers." He turned to Pop. "I can tell by the look on her face that we're grateful to take you up on such a fine offer."

He stood there for a minute considering things. "You know, for months on end, I have been having more bad luck than any one man should have to endure." He reached out to take her hand. "But lately I'm having more good luck than any man has a right to expect. I guess it evens out."

"Yes," Candace said. "Now, Reverend Green is still in town, I think we need to go see about planning a wedding."

He got a broad grin his face. "And it just keeps getting better."

About the Author

Terry writes Christian fiction with a western flair. He likes to say he is a "fifth generation Irish story teller and a fourth generation Texas teller of tall tales. Telling stories comes as natural as breathing and his stories reflect growing up helping Gene and Roy clean up the west in Saturday morning matinees. He has more than 40 books in print, most recently co-writing a primer for Christian writers entitled Writing in Obedience with editorial assistant Linda Yezak, and a Young Adult book entitled Beyond the Smoke, which won the Will Rogers Medallion. His faith is evident in his stories that his western writing friends call "Christian westerns," such as the three book Mysterious Ways series from David C. Cook. A bookstore of his available works as well as a periodic blog can be found at www.terryburns.net.